Harlequin Horse

Harlequin

VAN NOSTRAND REINHOLD COMPANY

NEW YORK · CINCINNATI · TORONTO · LONDON · MELBOURNE

Horse

Suzanne Wilding

VAN NOSTRAND REINHOLD COMPANY REGIONAL OFFICES:
CINCINNATI • NEW YORK • CHICAGO • MILLBRAE • DALLAS

VAN NOSTRAND REINHOLD COMPANY FOREIGN OFFICES:
LONDON • TORONTO • MELBOURNE

PUBLISHED BY VAN NOSTRAND REINHOLD COMPANY
450 WEST 33RD STREET, NEW YORK, N.Y. 10001

PUBLISHED SIMULTANEOUSLY IN CANADA BY
D. VAN NOSTRAND COMPANY (CANADA), LTD.

1 3 5 7 9 11 13 15 16 14 12 10 8 6 4 2

Book design by Lynn Hatfield

Printed and bound by Van Rees Book Company

1507072

This book is dedicated to the memory of another Granny whose most fervent wish was to be needed.

1

Wendy Fleming opened one eye, yawned, and rolled over. This was bliss. No rising bell, no studying—exams were over. She was home from boarding school and her own bed felt mighty comfortable. She moved her foot and accidentally poked Bitsy, her fat dachshund. Bitsy groaned and snuggled up closer.

"If you didn't hog the whole bed, I wouldn't kick you," Wendy said. Then she turned over to try to go back to sleep.

"Aren't you ever going to get up?" Robin's voice penetrated Wendy's pleasant waking dream.

Robin stormed into the room, tried to pull back the covers, and began to lecture. "Don't just lie there. Do something!" There was an air of urgency in her voice. Wendy opened an eye and looked at her younger sister. If she'd ever bother to run a comb through her brown hair and occasionally wash her pixieish face, she'd be pretty. "Little Tornado," as the family called her, was too thin, but to Wendy, constantly fighting the battle of the pounds, this was a cause for envy.

Grudgingly, Wendy opened both eyes. Slowly her comfortable room came into focus. The overstuffed furniture was shabby around the edges, the carpet still showed signs of Bitsy's puppyhood accidents, but the silver horse show trophies gleamed and the rows of ribbons, some slightly faded, were neatly strung behind the bookcase.

Robin, who had settled herself astride the desk chair, looked disapprovingly at the scrambled up sheets, and said, "Sleeping all day is not the way to find yourself a horse."

"Well, what do you suggest?" Wendy asked. "Should we look under a bush?"

It was easy for Robin to talk, Wendy thought sourly. She had Georgetown to ride as well as the run of their neighbor's stable. Wendy had once had a good pony, but Mr. Darling had long since been outgrown. Maybe she should have taken the camp job again. There was really nothing for her to do at Applebee Farm.

"Janie and I've been thinking . . ."

"Do you ever do anything without the Tweeds?" Wendy interrupted.

Janie Tweed was Robin's best friend. She was a good enough kid Wendy had to admit, but in her own horseless state the Tweeds bothered her. They had too much of everything, especially horses.

"Not often. If you'd stop being so grumpy and listen, we might be able to help." Robin's patience was wearing thin. "We've heard that Mrs. Perry needs someone to work her ponies. They're pretty young and green, but it would mean you'd be able to ride."

"Hey, that's a thought worth getting up for. I'll step on it." Wendy hopped out of bed and disappeared into the bathroom. A few moments later she called to Robin for help.

"Drat! I've dropped my contact lens. That's the third one I've lost this year."

Robin joined the search. "Where were you standing when it slipped?"

"Right next to the mirror."

Robin took one look and spied the wastebasket next to the basin. "Bet it fell in there. Let's turn it upside down."

Sure enough the costly lens was stuck in the wicker. Wendy gingerly disentangled it with some tweezers. "Thank goodness!" She put both lenses back in their case, took out her regular glasses, and slammed the drawer shut. Getting used to her contacts had been a misery, and now that her eyes were adjusted to them, their mortality rate was high.

"Don't forget we're going for your driver's permit this morning," her mother called.

Wendy brightened up considerably.

"But what about Mrs. Perry? You said you'd phone her," Robin insisted.

"I'll call her the moment I get back," Wendy promised. "Zip me up, Rob. I musn't be late." And for once Wendy stepped on it.

Mother and daughter drove through the Westchester countryside in comfortable silence as they passed the lush green fields, small patches of woodland, fancy gateposts to large estates, and here and there a small housing development. They were heading for the Bureau of Motor Vehicles in Carmel, New York. They had been told that usually the up-country bureau was not busy, and that there would be no waiting line.

When Mrs. Fleming and Wendy walked into the dull, brown painted room, two of the three officials were free.

"Do you have proof of age?" asked the woman at one window, without looking up from the form she was studying.

Wendy pulled out her birth certificate. The woman checked to see that Wendy was sixteen, and then handed her a form. In a bored tone of voice she said, "Fill it out completely. It'll cost you $2.50."

Mrs. Fleming and her daughter read the questions in fine print—name, address, age, weight, color of eyes and hair, and whether she had ever been in trouble with the law. Wendy filled in every space, signed on the dotted line, and returned it to the window. Her mother gave her the money, and Wendy disappeared into the next room to take her written test and eye examination.

Margaret Fleming waited a little anxiously. She reminded herself that this was routine. Wendy had studied the manual and would come through with flying colors. She only needed sixteen out of twenty correct answers to pass. That should be duck soup for a student as good as Wendy. Mrs. Fleming would have to see that her daughter had enough driving practice before they made the appointment for her final test.

It was getting hot, and she hoped Wendy would not take too much longer. Like Robin, Mrs. Fleming was intense, time conscious, and businesslike. She looked at her watch. Wendy had been gone twenty-five minutes.

What could she be doing? She was about to check up when Wendy appeared, hardly able to hold back tears.

"I couldn't pass the eye test," she said in a small voice. "The lady says I should come back with different glasses. They make you look into a machine called an Ortho-Rater," said Wendy, sniffling slightly. "I was great on the road signs and the color blindness test, but I just couldn't read the numbers and letters. I sure picked the wrong day to mess up my contacts."

"These things do happen," her mother said understandingly. Margaret Fleming was not going to scold Wendy at a time like this.

Nothing ever works for me, thought Wendy as she struggled with her boots. Even they were too tight.

Robin would say her muscles had gone flabby, and Wendy knew it was true. She threw her boots into the corner and put on her old sneakers. For what she was going to do they were good enough.

The call to Mrs. Perry about working her ponies had proved fruitless. The local riding stable had been even less encouraging. All that was left was to try to get into shape on her parents' old horses. At least riding them might tighten her leg muscles.

Mom had placed some cold cereal and milk on the kitchen table and Wendy sat down to eat a solitary breakfast.

Robin had conveniently left *The Chronicle* on the kitchen table. It was the horseman's bible, and Wendy studied the ads carefully. There were plenty of horses for sale, but that wouldn't help. There was little money around to buy anything, let alone horses. All the Flemings were horse crazy, but as is always the case when people are forced to economize, luxuries such as riding are the first to go.

Dad had recently had serious business reverses, and the way Mom talked it was hard enough to pay boarding school bills. Buying a new horse was out of the question. Every night now Dad brought home a briefcase bulging with work. He'd pore over its contents, make copious notes, and look even more grim when finished.

Little Tornado Robin had managed to solve her problem. She had helped Janie Tweed learn to ride, but that seemed little in exchange for having Papa Tweed give her a good pony like Georgetown.

In the mood Wendy was in, the cereal tasted like sawdust. Skipping breakfast would certainly do no harm, she decided. Like many girls her age, she was a little heavy and often, especially after just having finished a good meal, she promised herself to go on a diet. Wendy dumped her dishes in the sink, banged the kitchen door shut, and plodded down to the stable.

Foxy and Hippo, her parents' old horses, held no great fascination for her. They were "has-beens"; what she wanted was a horse of Georgetown's caliber. She was the oldest and she was tired of Robin getting all the breaks.

2

The Flemings' stable looked run-down and badly in need of paint, but even so, Wendy thought, there was no need for dirty bedding.

Get the lead out of your tail and you'll feel better. She repeated Robin's favorite piece of advice to herself as she grabbed a pitchfork and started to clean out Foxy's and Hippo's stalls. It looked as if no one had touched their home in months. Georgetown's stall was spotless, but Robin was undoubtedly too busy rushing over to the Tweeds' to give the older horses a thought.

I'll give her an earful the next time she tells me I'm lazy, Wendy thought as she worked. The weather was warm and June-like, the stable smelled pleasantly of horses, and she did not really object to mucking out. Slowly her anger began to subside. Her mother always said she'd rather clean a stall than make a bed, and her daughters felt the same way.

When the stalls were knee-deep in straw and the water buckets scrubbed and refilled, Wendy was satisfied. She took a lead shank from the hook and a measure full of oats and walked down to the pasture. She stopped at the gate, stuck two fingers in her mouth, and whistled. The old horses pricked up their ears, turned, and jogged to the gate. Wendy put the shank around Foxy's neck and Hippo followed.

At the sight of them Wendy's heart sank. They were both swaybacked and completely out of condition. Their coats were matted, their manes unkempt, and their feet needed trimming. Where had she ever gotten the idea that she might be able to get them into good enough shape to join Robin and Janie on their daily rides? Should she put them back in the pasture and return to bed, or should she give them a try? The thought of Robin's scorn made her go on. I'll clean both of them, see which is the sounder, and take a short ride.

Robin had mentioned that the horse vacuum cleaner was still working—that would help. She pulled the clumsy machine out of the tack room, plugged it in, and started running it over Foxy's coat. No rug was ever as dirty. The big horse liked the feel of the machine and stood quietly while Wendy vacuumed. Hippo's turn came next. He was a little ticklish under his tummy and stamped his foot in protest.

"Poor Hippo! I know you don't like the vacuum, but you're much too dirty for a brushing. Bear up! It will be over soon."

Hippo pinned his ears back and looked vicious. But that was all.

Wendy wetted a brush, smoothed down the horses'

straggly manes and tails, cleaned their feet with a hoof pick, and surveyed her charges. "You look much better," she said.

Under a cover in the tack room she found her saddle. The leather was well oiled and soft. Robin must have taken care of that. But the bridle was in sad shape. It hadn't been touched in a year and felt as if it would crack at the slightest pull.

She slipped the stiff leather over Foxy's big head. Then she placed the saddle on his sagging back, and walked him to the mounting block. Like the good old horse he was, Foxy stood and waited for his rider to climb aboard. Wendy put her left foot in the stirrup and swung herself into the saddle. It felt mighty strange. She hadn't ridden since she was at camp last summer.

She remembered to check the girth, and then their mutual conditioning began. Wendy felt like going out for a good ride, but she knew that Foxy wasn't up to it. It would take six weeks of slow work if he could be gotten back in shape at all. It was not a very exciting prospect.

Wendy sat up straight in the saddle. She tried to get her legs in position, but he was so big and fat that she perched like a jockey on top of his withers. Fortunately, Foxy never took a wrong step, but even his normal walk felt rolling and camel-like. On the way home Wendy tried a little trot. The gelding's stride was so short and choppy that she soon gave up. Of course Foxy was barefoot, but all the shoes in the world would not have made him sound. Wendy now understood why Mom had not been able to find a home for them. Hippo might be better, but she doubted it.

She unsaddled the old horse and put him in his stall.

Tacking up Hippo, she climbed on his back and walked out to the field. Even at a walk she realized that he was unsound and decided not to trot him. Tired, dirty, and thoroughly discouraged, she returned to the stable yard. I can clean my tack and kiss the idea of ever riding with Robin and Janie good-bye, she thought. Wendy swallowed hard as she rubbed glycerine soap into her Pariani saddle. At least it was still good. But why hang on to it? Her riding days were finished.

I might as well forget about horses and try earning some money. Walkers' in White Plains hires school and college girls in their junior dress department. If I could land a job there, I'd at least keep busy and be able to buy my winter clothes at a discount.

She was so preoccupied with her thoughts that she did not hear the bright red sports car turn into the yard until it ground to a halt. A new Austin-Healey at Applebee Farm! It must belong to the Tweeds, she thought grumpily, as she wiped her soapy hands on her jeans, stuffed her shirt tail into her pants, and went out to investigate.

Sitting at the wheel of the car was the sloppiest looking girl Wendy had ever seen. Her hair was black and stringy. Her face, set in a disgruntled scowl, was badly in need of a wash. As for her clothes, it had been weeks since they had seen the inside of a washing machine. What was someone who looked like this doing in such a posh car?

The girl sat in the convertible acting as if the stable yard was hers. She looked vaguely familiar, but Wendy couldn't place the enormous, square sun glasses, the sloppy poor boy sweater, and ragged jeans.

"Aren't any of the Flemings around?" she asked. She

then lit a cigaret, tossed the match over her shoulder, and made herself comfortable.

Wendy wondered just who this creature thought she was talking to.

"I'm Wendy Fleming."

"You?"

Wendy couldn't believe that one short word could sound so rude.

"My name is Muriel Alexander." She paused to let the news sink in.

It registered. Wendy wanted to say, "You must be the owner of Harlequin." But instead she said formally, "How do you do. What can I do for you?"

"For *me!*" Muriel Alexander laughed and flicked ashes into the yard. "Nothing, but I might be able to help you."

"You must be mistaken." Wendy bristled noticeably. She had had her fill of this character. "Perhaps you're looking for the Tweeds' place."

"Oh, no! You're the girl who wants a horse, aren't you?"

Wendy nodded.

"Well, I'm looking for a home for a very good one. I'm sick of horses. I want to own one of these babies," she said, giving her shiny red conveyance an appreciative glance.

"Who owns this?" asked Wendy.

Muriel patted the leather upholstery lovingly. "This belongs to Terrence Van Horn III, and he won't let me drive it for long."

"I *am* looking for a horse, but I can't buy one. I still think you want to see the Tweeds." This girl is waving a carrot in front of my nose, she thought bitterly. She turned her back on Miss Temptation and busied herself patting Foxy's head.

"I hear you take excellent care of your horses, and that you're a good rider." Muriel talked girl-to-girl now. She seemed to have seen that her attitude was getting her nowhere. "We can help each other," she said earnestly, and for the first time looked Wendy straight in the eye. "My parents are sick of paying board on a horse that I don't ride. If I can get them off the hook for a while, they might buy me a car."

"What's that to me?" Wendy was trying not to let her longing get the better of her.

"I'm offering you Harlequin. If you will take care of him ... for the summer at least," she added as an afterthought.

"Harlequin! You must be joking."

3

Wendy had decided to wait until lunch was over before she broke the big news, but not talking about Harlequin, even for an hour, was more difficult than she expected.

Wendy loved to eat, and her waistline showed it, but today she was much too excited to appreciate her mother's best cheese omelet and strawberry shortcake.

Robin, noticing her lack of appetite inquired, "What's up?"

Wendy shook her head. She did not trust her voice.

She watched as Dad popped the last strawberry into his mouth, sat back, and lit his pipe. Then, Wendy cleared her throat and announced, "I have some great news." Her voice sounded tense.

Mrs. Fleming stopped in the middle of folding her napkin. Her father took the pipe out of his mouth. Wendy saw how tired and preoccupied he looked. But she felt sure that when he heard what she had to say, he would be happy for her.

"I've found a horse," she told them breathlessly. Her eyes sparkled and her crooked Fleming grin lighting up her whole face.

"You've *what?*" Robin exclaimed.

"A horse . . . where?" Mom was plainly puzzled.

"Suppose we let Wendy tell us about it," Dad said, and pushed his chair back. He relit his pipe, and settled down to listen. He was anxious to hear about Wendy's good fortune. Anticipating his wife's next move he said, "The dishes can wait, Margaret."

"Well, it was like this . . ." Wendy blurted out the story of Muriel Alexander, the red sports car, and Harlequin.

"Harlequin! That's a terrific horse," Robin said, with surprise. "He cleaned up last year. Why would Muriel Alexander be . . ." She stopped short.

Dad sucked on his pipe looking worried, but Mom came out with it. "Why would the Alexanders lend you a horse with Harlequin's reputation? There would be no problem selling him."

"Mom . . ." Wendy pleaded. She knew her mother was right, but she did not want her bubble to burst this soon. "The Alexanders are spending $150 a month board at Rocking Horse Farm on an animal that Muriel isn't riding. Can't you see that they'd like to get off the hook? Muriel thinks they'll buy her a car if Harlequin's board is taken off their hands."

"I can see all that, Wen." Her mother came over and put her arms around her daughter. "But why then don't they sell the horse for a good price?" Mrs. Fleming wanted to see her girl happy, but she was too practical to believe in miracles.

"Well, he is quite old," Wendy began. "And they know we would take care of him," she ended with a rush. Even to her, the argument sounded weak. She looked to her father for support. Dad as a rule was not as suspicious of people. Mom was the cynic of the family.

"It does sound too good to be true, Wen," Mr. Fleming said. "But I see absolutely no harm in investigating the whole proposition."

Wendy bounced out of her chair and threw herself into her father's arms. It was like years ago when he used to comfort her after she had fallen off Mr. Darling. He had a way of making everyone feel better. "Let's start right away," she whispered to him. "I can't wait to bring Harley home."

"You call Mrs. Alexander," he instructed his wife. "We need to know if Muriel told Wendy the straight story."

"We'll do the dishes," Robin volunteered. She had a knack of knowing when a diversion was necessary. "Nothing like washing a stack of cups and plates to kill the suspense."

"You'd better stick to the pots and pans," Robin instructed her sister once they were out of earshot. "In the state you're in, I wouldn't trust you with anything breakable."

Wendy, who usually objected violently to pot slinging, grinned. "Guess you're right," she admitted, as she wiped out the omelet pan. Might as well keep busy she told herself grudgingly. Mom doesn't like people breathing down her neck when she's telephoning.

Mrs. Alexander corroborated Muriel's story but Mrs.

Fleming was still not convinced. "Muriel's mother has agreed to let us take the horse," she told her husband, then turning to Wendy she said, "but please don't set your heart on Harlequin. This may turn out to be only a temporary arrangement."

"You're just an old crepe-hanger," Wendy told her mother kiddingly. "Why can't I be lucky for once?"

"I'll keep all my fingers and toes crossed," her mother promised.

The Tweeds were most amiable about lending their horse trailer. "Keep it at your place," Harry Tweed suggested. "Now that he have a van, we hardly ever use it."

The drive to Rocking Horse Farm was great. For once Dad forgot about the disastrous oil prospecting scheme his firm had become involved in, and sang at the top of his voice. He was the only member of the Fleming clan who could carry a tune, but Wendy joined in the encore of "Home on the Range."

"Must you?" Robin held her hands over her ears. "I can't stand anymore."

"Okay, I'll shut up." Wendy sat the rest of the way obligingly silent. Then suddenly she burst out, "Dad, will you teach me how to drive the trailer? That is, after I get my driver's license?"

"When's your oculist appointment?" her Father asked, suddenly turning serious. He was bothered about Wendy's eyes. One only needed 20-40 vision to pass an eye test and Wendy had failed it.

"Monday," she said, and seeing her father's worried expression, she added, "Don't give it a thought, Dad. I wouldn't have flunked the test with contact lenses. The glasses I wore were antiques."

"You'd better drive for a while before you attempt a trailer," her father told her. "These babies jackknife if you're not careful. They're definitely not toys." On that sobering note they arrived at Rocking Horse Farm.

The place looked deserted. Most of the adults rode in the morning, and Felix, the instructor-manager, and the kids were at a horse show.

In the third barn Wendy found an old groom. He looked disagreeable and smelled of whiskey. "We've come to fetch Harlequin," she told him brightly.

"Harlequin, Harlequin," he repeated woozily. He scratched his head and thought a minute, "That is the white-faced horse?"

Wendy nodded happily.

"You're welcome to him. He's nothin' but a bother. . . ."

"Why is he a bother?" Mr. Fleming had followed Wendy into the barn.

The old man looked up, studied Mr. Fleming carefully, and decided that there might be a tip in it for him. "He's a cribber, he's a poor doer, and he pigs up his stall. He'll crib on a bloody toothpick," he added maliciously.

"Cribbing is a nuisance," Mr. Fleming allowed, "but sucking air while chewing on any hard surface is a habit many good horses have."

"Why, even Kelso cribs," Robin volunteered, "and he was race horse of the year for five straight seasons and won close to two million dollars."

"As to your other complaints, a little good stable management might solve those," Mr. Fleming said, looking sternly at the groom. "Now, if you will tell us where the horse is, we'll take him home."

Wendy gave her father a grateful look.

The groom walked ahead, muttering to himself. In the farthest stall of the farthest barn he stopped, threw open the door, and pointed. "He's all yours," he mumbled. "Good riddance!"

It took the Flemings a few seconds to get used to the dim light. All three of them stood and stared at Harlequin.

Robin spoke first. "He's the picture of a white-faced Hereford."

"He's quite a looker!" Mr. Fleming said, letting out a low whistle.

Wendy seemed to be holding her breath. Finally she stammered, "He's . . . he's . . . beautiful!" She could hardly take her eyes off the bright chestnut with the four white stockings and the white, white face.

"Why, he has blue eyes, white eye lashes, and a pink nose," Robin said as she danced around the old horse. "He looks just like a white faced cow."

"He's my horse now," Wendy said defensively turning to her sister. "Remember, you are speaking of the horse who won ten junior working hunter championships last year." Then she slipped a halter over his head, patted his neck gently, and walked him out to the trailer.

The groom followed after them muttering to himself:

"One white foot, buy him.
Two white feet, try him.
Three white feet, look well about him.
Four white feet, do without him."

Wendy was too thrilled to listen. Mr. Fleming was reserving judgment. Only Robin was her usual teasing self. "Good thing we don't have the steers anymore. Harley would always be getting mixed up with them."

Wendy gave her pesty sister a swift kick on the shins. "Mind your own business," she said as Robin yelped. She led Harlequin into the trailer. The old horse followed obediently, and stood quietly while she tied him up, and they closed the tail gate.

"Home, James!" Wendy gave her father a kiss and settled herself next to him on the front seat of the Ford.

4

"You need a good cleaning," Wendy said, and eyed her new charge critically. "Rocking Horse Farm doesn't do much for their $150 a month, do they?"

As if in agreement, Harlequin snorted and nuzzled Wendy's hand. He like being fussed over and had received little personal attention in months.

After a few days at Applebee Farm Harlequin's chestnut coat looked brighter and his skin appeared less tightly drawn over his bony frame. But Wendy was a good enough horsewoman to know that it would take months to get his normal weight back.

"You're going to get your stockings washed," she told him one morning during his first week at Applebee Farm. Harlequin eyed the bucket of warm soapy water suspiciously. With a little encouragement from his new mistress, he stuck one hoof at a time into the pail.

"Not bad, is it, old boy?" she murmured reassuringly as she scrubbed.

After all four of Harlequin's legs had been cleaned, Wendy stepped back to admire him. "You're beginning to look like a classy horse again. With regular exercise and lots of good groceries..." Wendy stopped in mid-sentence and looked suddenly serious. She was feeding Harlequin more than Georgetown, Foxy, and Hippo put together. Grain and hay were expensive. She would have to earn plenty to pay the additional costs.

"But that's not your problem," she said, and patted Harlequin on the rump. She hurried to find her saddle and bridle. "All you have to do is win at horse shows."

Robin had called him a paint pony. "Papers or no, he can't be a thoroughbred," she had insisted. But Rob was just jealous. Wendy was sure of that.

His bridle adjusted and his girth tight, Wendy mounted her horse and began humming to herself as she rode out into the pasture. Robin had christened it the jump field (to keep up with the Tweeds, Wendy figured), but in reality it was nothing but Foxy's and Hippo's pasture with a few jumps added.

The old horse stepped out, his white lashes flickering, his limpid blue eyes surveying the scenery. He seemed glad to be working again, and he reacted well to Wendy's light touch. "We'll get fit together," she promised him. They walked around the field once. Then she crossed her stirrups over the pommel of the saddle and urged Harlequin to trot slowly. "This'll help our leg muscles."

Harlequin's trot was springy, and it was not easy to keep her legs in contact with the horse. Get your heels down, she told herself. You have to tighten your seat.

Ten minutes of sitting trot was all Wendy could take. Her legs felt raw under her blue jeans, and her back ached in the most surprising places. She picked up her stirrups and let Harlequin catch his breath. Then she started to canter. Foxy and Hippo stopped grazing and looked up in mild astonishment. They were not used to seeing Wendy and that white-faced horse working around their field.

Harlequin may have had the coloring of a paint pony, but he was a thoroughbred, and his strides ate up the ground. He enjoyed stretching his legs, and Wendy loved the feeling of speed. She wished Robin could see them as she stood up in her stirrups and let him run. The wind pulled at her hair and tore at her worn shirt.

After three laps Wendy was tired but Harley was still going strong. She eased her weight back into the saddle and took a firm hold on the reins, expecting him to stop, but Harlequin tore on. It seemed as if they'd been galloping forever. Wendy tried to stop him again. She was really bushed now. Foxy and Hippo looked as if they might join the chase. That's all we need, thought Wendy worriedly.

Harlequin was tiring too, but like so many thoroughbreds, the more tired he became the more he leaned into the bit. His mouth has gone cold. He can't feel me pulling. Wendy was close to panic. Gathering all her strength, she set one rein on the horse's neck, and used the other as an emergency pulley rein. It worked. He slowed down immediately, and she managed to circle him to a halt.

"You do get the bit between your teeth, don't you!" she said as she gasped for breath. Harley breathed hard and coughed. He was covered with sweat.

"A good mouth is not one of your assets. But tomorrow we'll take a few jumps and see whether you're really as terrific as they say you are." Wendy walked more than twenty minutes to cool out her race horse and then took him back to the stable.

"Are you and that noisy white-faced cow ready? We have a date with Janie at eleven," said Robin the following morning.

Wendy had wasted no time teaching Harlequin to recognize her footsteps. "The sugar treatment," she called it. After a few days, as soon as she neared the stable, the old horse would neigh a welcome.

"He'll learn to nip," Robin warned correctly, but Wendy only laughed.

"Let him," she agreed amiably. "He can use plenty of T.L.C., and I intend to give it to him."

Wendy lugged her saddle out of the tack room. She hadn't had a chance to clean it since her escapade, and it was caked with sweat.

"How did you get your Pariani so filthy?" asked Robin eyeing the saddle suspiciously.

"Well, you know he isn't very fit and ... I haven't cleaned it since yesterday," Wendy finished lamely. She was not going to talk about Harlequin's race in the pasture.

"Come on!" Robin did not give the dirty tack another thought. "Janie doesn't like to wait."

Wendy hustled and without too much delay was ready to follow her sister.

Harlequin moved sedately. He had gotten the run out of himself yesterday and was ready to settle down. "I'll lead," Wendy told Robin. She wasn't going to let George start cantering and have Harley take off after him.

They crossed the road, and as they started to trot down the grassy lane the full impact of her good fortune flooded over her. She shut her eyes. If she pinched herself, would she wake up and find that it was just a dream? She touched Harley's warm neck. She was on a live horse, *that* was reassuring. Wendy ignored her aching muscles and sat up very straight. She must keep the chestnut at his normal springy trot. "No racing today," she told him severely.

"Harlequin certainly has a long stride. George has to canter to keep up with him," Robin said, with a touch of envy in her voice.

"George moves like a little horse, not like a choppy pony," Wendy said magnanimously. She had her own thoroughbred now, but would she be able to jump him? Suddenly it all seemed too good to be true.

The two girls walked their horses down the lane and through the Tweeds' pastures. Robin could not keep her eyes off Harlequin. His markings are funny, she thought to herself, and his watch eyes may take a little getting used to, but when he moves he is a stunner. If he jumps half as well as they say, he'll be terrific. There's no reason to be jealous though. George is wonderful. But she continued to look admiringly at the flashy chestnut.

"I wouldn't overdo it today," Robin counseled out loud. "Remember that Harley isn't fit."

"And neither am I!" Wendy said, and laughed a trifle nervously. "I haven't jumped a fence since camp." They were in the Tweeds' jump field now, and the obstacles looked imposing.

Chubby Janie Tweed and her equally fat pony Snooks, were busily chugging over a series of parallel poles lying a few inches above the ground. These cavallettis were used as an exercise for jumping. Sit-trotting through the evenly spaced rails was good for both horse and rider. The girls had made it a part of their morning routine, and usually, nothing could turn Janie off. Suddenly she stopped and stared at Harlequin. She let out a low whistle, giving him the once over as she circled around. Finally she said, "That's quite a horse. I like him." Coming from plump, pig-tailed Janie, that was a great compliment.

Janie Tweed was as short as Robin was tall, as plump as her friend was thin, and as carefree as Robin was serious. Opposites attract, Wendy thought, and in this case it seemed true.

"Come join us," Robin called, and Wendy trotted over to the cavallettis.

"He's probably never seen anything like this," Harlequin's mistress warned. But the white-faced thoroughbred moved through the poles as if he had done it all his life.

At the end of the six cavallettis Robin put up a small post-and-rail. Janie's pony Snooks hopped over it, and so did George, but Harlequin had to twist. The spacing was too close for him.

"That's enough of that," Wendy decided. She looked around for a more suitable obstacle.

"The brush," Robin suggested, and Wendy headed for it. Horses usually jump fences made of greenery well, and the Tweeds' brush was particularly attractive. It was a three-feet six-inch privet hedge.

Wendy noticed a tight feeling in her stomach as she steered toward the jump. As she let Harlequin break into a canter, she forced her heels down and her eyes up, and rode a straight line. Just before the jump, she squeezed and Harlequin took off.

The horse took a beautiful fence, but Wendy was left on the "back porch," behind the motion of the horse. Her feet stuck out in front of her and her fanny bounced on Harley's kidneys.

"You asked and then didn't go with him," Robin yelled. "He gave you a beautiful jump and you jabbed him in the mouth. You can't treat a good horse like that!"

"It was terrible," Wendy agreed. But under her breath she said, "You needn't rub it in." She headed for the same jump again, but this time as she asked Harlequin to take off she grabbed a little piece of mane and stayed in position. Both of them took it well.

"That was better," Janie called. "He sure can jump when you give him half a chance." Janie took advantage of the lull, smacked Snooks on the rump and headed into the first of a series of little jumps. Snooks resented the stick and let out a good buck. Janie's short legs never had a chance and she fell off. As this was an everyday occurrence, Janie picked herself up, brushed off the seat of her pants, and climbed aboard again.

Janie now tackled the cross-rails without stirrups while Robin and George practiced over the in-and-out. Wendy patted her horse and decided to catch her breath. She held it when she was nervous, and the two jumps had left her gasping.

Harlequin stopped, turned his head and looked at the

girl in the saddle. How about some sugar, he seemed to say.

"You beggar!" Wendy leaned forward and handed him a grubby piece. "You don't have to slobber all over me," she complained good naturedly as she wiped her hands in his mane.

Harlequin, chewing happily, condescended to walk.

I'll take the course once, Wendy figured, and whether it's good or bad, I'll stop. I don't want to overdo it on the first day.

The Tweeds had built a model horse show course. They had planted evergreens on either side of the natural wood obstacles, and potted geraniums added color to the chicken coop and white gate. It was both picturesque and practical as it was laid out with a high and a low side, for horses and ponies, respectively. Wendy was planning to take the high side.

Out of the corner of one eye she could see Robin and Janie standing like judges in the center of the field.

"We'll show 'em," she whispered to Harlequin as she gathered up the reins and eased her willing horse into a canter. They circled once and negotiated the brush faultlessly. Then they turned toward the Millbrook—a fence made up of a series of rails, one on top of the other. Harlequin turned well and headed into the jump. Wendy remembered to put her hand in his mane and they sailed over. The chicken coop came next. Harley hesitated a moment, but Wendy clucked to give him encouragement. They cleared it with six inches to spare. Next, came the white gate. They were cantering downhill now, and Harlequin tried to roll on, but Wendy sat up straight in her saddle and steadied her horse. However, he did get rolling and hit the gate out of stride. It could have been bad, but Harlequin corrected himself and twisted only slightly. Wendy relaxed. She knew now that he could jump anything. The only problem was to keep him slow enough to meet his fences correctly. They arrived in stride at the post-and-rail and ended with a spectacular in-and-out jump.

"Wow!" Wendy said. She dropped the reins on Harlequin's neck, and the old horse pulled up by himself. He seemed glad for the chance to rest. The course was a long one for his unused muscles.

Wendy hopped off and put her arms around him. She buried her head on his sweaty shoulder and said, "You're every bit as good as they said you were." Then she loosened his girth and found another piece of sugar for him.

For a few moments Robin and Janie were stunned, then they swarmed all over her.

"That was great! That was terrific!"

"If he'll go like that at the show, you've got it made!"

Janie thumped Wendy on the back. "You're even better than Robin on Georgetown!" she said enthusiastically. And to Janie that was almost an impossibility.

It had been a long time since Wendy had heard such praise and it sounded good. She let Robin finish her workout, and then both of them started back for the farm.

She felt as though she was dreaming as she put her marvelous horse to bed, cleaned the tack, and returned to the house.

As the girls walked onto the back porch, they heard Mom on the telephone. "She's using her Aunt Ruth voice," whispered Robin wickedly. Their father's sister talked endlessly on the phone, and they could tell when she had Mom hog-tied.

"You've been over the whole story three times," they heard their mother say. "I hope you're wrong, but I'll look into it." There was a pause and then Mrs. Fleming added, "Yes, I'll have Harlequin's eyes and lungs checked, and I won't let Wendy jump him before Dr. Wallace gives his okay."

Robin grabbed Wendy's hand. "Don't you believe a word of it," she insisted. "You know what a troublemaker Aunt Ruth is. She doesn't know what she is talking about. A horse that can't see or has lung trouble couldn't perform the way Harlequin did this morning."

Robin looked at Wendy's pale face, but her older sister did not seem to hear her. "It'll all work out fine," she promised.

Wendy responded gratefully to the squeeze, but she said nothing. She could not trust her voice.

5

Mom put down the receiver and turned to Wendy.

"Dr. Wallace is speaking at a veterinarian's convention in Chicago and won't return until Wednesday," she said. "There's nothing to do but wait until he gets back."

Wendy looked at her small, oh so well organized mother. How could she be calm about something that was so desperately important? How could she go on as if nothing had happened? Didn't she know that this was the worst thing ever? Mom had made much more fuss about her failing the eye test. Didn't she understand what was at stake? Wendy wanted to yell and throw things, but instead she ran to her room and slammed the door.

Downstairs, George Fleming gave vent to his feelings. "Drat Ruth!" He banged his fist on the desk. "She has to spoil the first nice thing that has happened to Wen in ages."

"Your fuming isn't going to help a bit. Ruth mostly listens to only half a story and then makes up the rest." Over the years Margaret Fleming had learned to cope with her sister-in-law. Mrs. Fleming was the coolest member of the family, but for once she didn't feel as confident as she sounded.

"I wish I could buy her a horse," Mr. Fleming said under his breath, but then pulling himself together he asked, "What did Ruth actually say was wrong with the horse?"

"Ruth heard rumors that the Alexanders couldn't sell Harlequin because his eyesight was marginal and getting worse and his lungs were in awful shape. There could be some truth in it. I've heard Harlequin cough, and I've never seen eyes like his before." Now it was Mom's turn to bang the drawer shut.

Wendy opened her bedroom door and heard the end of the conversation. Mom *does* care, Wendy decided, even if she tries to sound so businesslike.

"Wednesday is only three days off," she listened to her father's temperate comment. "We'll get Dr. Wallace over the moment he gets back, and then we will know more of what we're talking about."

Upstairs, Wendy could not help the few tears that dampened her quilted bedspread. No one could complain if she cried in her own room.

But Robin did. She barged into her sister's room without knocking. "Stop feeling sorry for yourself and do something," she ordered. "I'm going down to feed Georgetown. Are you going to let Harley starve?"

Wendy turned her head to the wall. She thought she wanted to be alone, but Bitsy, her dachshund, knew better.

He snuggled up and licked her nose. "Go away!" she ordered, but Bitsy knew that she didn't mean it.

What if Aunt Ruth were right? What if there was something very wrong with Harley? That would explain Muriel's amazing generosity.

As if guessing her thoughts, Robin interrupted. "Muriel's a fink! She showed quite a bit last year and when she didn't win she acted terrible." Robin plopped herself on the bed. "Do you remember what she did at the Secor Show?"

Wendy shook her head. "I wasn't home that weekend."

"Well, she and Harlequin had a good round in the Junior Working Hunters until they reached the last fence. He took one of his tremendous leaps and Muriel landed on his kidneys with a thud. This made him hit the jump and knock the rail down. It was all her fault," Robin continued with obvious relish, "but Muriel was so furious that she started beating Harlequin. The judge yanked her off the horse and told Felix, her instructor, to send her home and never to show in front of him again."

Two days had passed since Aunt Ruth's phone call had ruined Wendy's dream. She tried to avoid the stable. Play it cool! Don't get more involved with Harley than you are already, the practical side of her nature warned her. If he was really dangerous to ride, her parents would certainly not let her keep him.

Harlequin, knowing nothing of the commotion he was causing, always welcomed the girls with a shrill whinny. Applebee Farm was his first real home.

Muriel Alexander had acquired him from a young man who was interested only in jumping. Everytime he rode he had asked the willing horse to take thirty or forty fences. When Muriel owned him she thought of him as a machine on which she could win horse show trophies. Probably, she had more feeling for her boy friend's red sports car than for her white-faced horse.

In the few days since Harlequin's arrival the stable atmosphere had changed. All four stalls were filled and the place was alive again. Two horses were working daily, two saddles and bridles were in use, and everywhere there were signs of activity. Not only were the stalls cleaner, but with Robin's assistance Wendy had refurbished the green and yellow tack room.

The dust sheets were neatly stashed away and the felt cloth covered the table once more. The girls polished up the trophies until they shone. Then they put Dad's hunting horn and whip in the proper place on the window sill and hung his sporting prints on the wall. As a final touch Wendy put the horsey slipcover back on the wing chair.

The two girls swept the yard, and surveyed their handiwork. Despite the peeling paint, Applebee Farm's stable was in business again.

Wendy patted her horse and slipped him a handful of sugar. While she cleaned his stall she talked to him. "I'll look after you, old sport, but I'm not going to ride you until after the vet's been here. I don't want to get to like you even more." She swallowed the lump in her throat, snapped a shank onto his halter, and led him down to Foxy's and Hippo's pasture.

Robin followed Wendy. The moment the older girl released the horse he galloped away, happy to be free. Soon he stopped, pawed the ground, and rolled like a colt.

Then he shook himself and started the serious business of grazing.

The girls watched him carefully. "There can't be anything wrong with those pretty blue eyes," Robin said, chewing a blade of grass. She tried to sound convincing. "Bet Aunt Ruth's just trying to make trouble."

"Hope so." Wendy stuck her hands in her jeans' pockets and walked hurriedly back to the house. She knew Robin meant well, but she didn't want to see her getting Georgetown ready to ride. That would be too hard to take.

Tuesday was Wendy's oculist appointment. She tried to joke about it as they drove to town. "Harlequin and I make a fine pair," she said. "We should have brought him with us. Perhaps Dr. Cook would examine both of us at a discount."

Mom failed to see the humor. "I don't understand why you flunked your eye test," she said. "Do you see better with contacts? Your regular glasses aren't that old."

"I think I do," but Wendy did not sound too convincing.

They parked the car, and after the usual forty-five minute wait, Dr. Cook saw them. Wendy knew the ropes. She sat down opposite the eye chart, looked through dozens of different lenses, and read endless rows of letters and numbers. Then the doctor put drops in her eyes and waited until the belladonna had dilated her pupils.

"If you had not worn five year old glasses to take your eye test for your learner's permit, you would never have had any trouble," was his verdict. "Your eyes are now accustomed to contact lenses. You cannot go back to weaker conventional glasses. I'll give you a new prescription for regular glasses if you want them. Otherwise use your contacts and you'll be fine."

"Do you really mean it?" Wendy could not believe her good fortune. If only Harlequin's problems would be as simple!

Applebee Farm was Dr. Wallace's first stop Wednesday morning. As he stepped out of his station wagon, heavily laden with supplies, the whole family was assembled to greet him. Everyone wanted to be present at Harlequin's physical.

Mr. Fleming, who had stayed home from the office, sucked on his pipe, and watched silently as Dr. Wallace took his medicine bag out of the car. George Fleming rarely took a day off but he wasn't going to miss this all important visit from the vet.

Margaret Fleming made a conscious effort to look cheerful and wide awake. The truth was that she had spent a sleepless night worrying about Wendy's summer. How was her oldest daughter going to spend her time if the vet corroborated Ruth's story?

"Bring the horse over here, girls," Dr. Wallace instructed.

Harlequin, as if knowing that his fate was at stake, pranced out of his stall like a two-year-old. "I've found a good home," he seemed to say.

Wendy made Harlequin stand square, his feet under him, his neck stretched, and his ears pricked.

Dr. Wallace wasted no time looking at the pretty picture. He opened Harlequin's mouth and looked at his teeth. "He's no youngster," was his only comment.

He went over his legs and carefully examined his bumps and lumps.

"He's got a splint the size of an egg on his near fore," Robin whispered to her mother.

"That's enough, Rob," her father said, sternly.

"If it's an old splint, it may never bother him," her mother answered.

Wendy pretended not to hear.

"Put a saddle and bridle on him, young lady, and let's see how he moves." The vet knew how badly Wendy wanted this horse. Sometimes it wasn't easy to remain professionally impartial.

It didn't take long to tack up Harlequin, but before Dr. Wallace let Wendy ride down to the pasture, he listened to the horse's heart. He would check again after Harlequin exercised. He also watched his sides. Some lung problems such as heaves are obvious.

"Jog him first," the doctor ordered. Wendy trotted in a big circle. Harlequin moved well. His three white stockings and his one white sock gleamed in the morning sun.

"What a beautiful stride!" commented Mr. Fleming, and his wife nodded in agreement.

"Canter," came the doctor's orders.

Wendy said a silent prayer as she let Harlequin slip into his smooth, effortless canter. She sat quietly, keeping a light feel of his mouth. He coughed once or twice but otherwise showed no distress.

"Let him gallop, and when I put my hand up, stop!"

"Did you hear that?" Wendy whispered to her horse as she shortened up on the reins and leaned forward slightly.

Harlequin responded, and soon they tore around the field.

"Stop!" called the doctor and the horse slowed down on his own. Wendy, remembering last week's race, was relieved. She came to a halt in front of Dr. Wallace, dropped the reins, and waited for orders. Harlequin, breathing hard, looked glad for the rest.

"He's not very fit," Wendy said apologetically.

"That's all right," said the doctor. He listened long and hard to the horse's heart with his stethoscope. Then he glanced at the heaving sides. The old horse coughed and the vet looked grave as he examined him.

Everyone waited silently. Finally Dr. Wallace broke the spell.

"Cool him out and then bring him to the stable. I need a dark place to check his eyes." He made no other comment.

As Wendy rode back to the stable she thought, my old riding instructor would have said, "No good will come of this." But she kept her head up and her shoulders back. There was a determined look on her face. Somehow it must all work out.

Robin carried the saddle and bridle to the tack room. By the time the doctor joined them in the stable the girls had sponged the horse's back and had made him comfortable.

Dr. Wallace picked the darkest corner of Harlequin's stall to start his eye examination. He took the ophthalmoscope out of its padded box and studied Harlequin's eyes carefully.

It seemed like forever. Finally Dr. Wallace put his instrument away, snapped shut the case, and walked back to his car. Wendy remained in Harlequin's stall, petting him.

"Wen, dear, the doctor wants to talk with us." Her mother's voice made her realize she must face whatever was coming.

"It's like this," Dr. Wallace began. He had stowed his gear and was ready to give his verdict.

"I haven't seen many thoroughbreds with two watch eyes," Dr. Wallace mused. "But in western horses it's commonplace."

"Is that what makes Harley's eyes pale blue?" Robin asked.

"Yes . . ." he hesitated a moment before explaining. "A watch eye is an eye in which the iris lacks pigment, making it appear bluish white in color." He paused.

Dad, leaning against the doctor's car refilled his pipe and puffed slowly. Mom was seated on the mounting block and she motioned Wendy to join her. Robin, sucking a blade of grass as usual, had propped herself against the stable door.

The doctor cleared his throat and continued. "How well do you like this horse?" he asked.

"I love him. He's wonderful." Wendy was surprised at how loud her voice sounded. Robin nodded in agreement. Their parents said nothing.

The old horse looked at the girls with his odd colored eyes. He's pleading with us. He wants to stay, Wendy thought. She didn't quite believe this, and yet. . . .

The doctor continued. "This is not a cut and dried case. If you were buying the horse and you asked me to pass him, I couldn't . . ."

"But we're not," Wendy interrupted.

"Is he safe?" was Mrs. Fleming's first question.

Wendy held her breath.

The doctor paused. "He is safe . . . if you use your head," he answered.

Dr. Wallace paced up and down and spoke thoughtfully. "The horse has heaves. As you know, heaves is a disease in which lung tissue breaks down. Every time he coughs hard another little piece breaks away, and his breathing gets worse. If you are willing to bed him down on peat moss, which is relatively dust free, feed him a prepared non-allergenic food, and give him no hay, you may arrest the disease. At worst you can slow it down immeasurably."

Wendy breathed again.

"But how about his sight," Mom insisted. "That's even more important."

"I was coming to that." The doctor chose his words carefully. "He definitely does not have perfect vision." He hated to say it, but that was his job.

"Is it very bad?" Wendy's question slipped out unintentionally.

"It may not be as bad as it sounds," the doctor answered kindly. "If you say he jumps as well as he does, he must be able to see adequately now. His sight may not deteriorate appreciably for years, or he may be blind within six months. That's the chance you will be taking."

Looking directly at the senior Flemings he said, "If the horse is as good as your daughter says, put him on New Hope Feed, turn him out as much as possible, and have his eyes checked regularly. If you watch him carefully, he'll tell you himself if his sight is bothering him."

Mr. Fleming nodded with relief. Wendy did not trust herself to speak. Robin recovered first. As soon as the vet's car had disappeared down the bumpy back drive, she said, "What are we waiting for? Let's go for a ride."

"May I?" Wendy looked hopefully at her mother.

"Yes, dear, I'll even tack up old Foxy and join you." For the moment at least the sun shone on Applebee Farm.

6

Whichever way she added it, the final figure was always the same—too high. Harlequin's monthly expenses were terrific! Wendy wrinkled her brow, chewed her pencil, and scowled at the itemized list she had made.

Feed	$30.00
Bedding	25.00
Shoeing	12.50
Vet and Misc.	25.00
	$92.50

How was she ever going to earn that much money? If she made ten dollars a week baby sitting, it would help. But where would she get the other fifty dollars? She shoved the pad in the table drawer, and tightened the belt on her blue jeans. Then she strode purposefully out of the tack room. Wendy absolutely refused to let finances spoil her day.

Harlequin's arrival had put a new meaning into her summer. She was busy, happy, and much thinner. Gone was what Robin called the "blubber of despondency." Wendy could not help being short, but she could, and did, cut out candy bars. Five pounds lighter, she looked trim and neat in her faded blue jeans and plaid shirt. Her hair, just released from a night of rollers, waved casually over her ears. Her eyes sparkled with the fun of being alive.

As Janie Tweed's older brother, Willy, drove into the Fleming's stable to visit Wendy, he noticed the changes in her. In fact he had been the first one to comment on a difference.

"Robin's sister sure has changed," he told Janie one morning over breakfast. "She used to be sort of dull and dumpy. Now she's quite a looker. She's really with it."

"Harlequin's changed her," said Janie, munching cereal.

A horse changing a girl? That was a new twist. But Janie wasn't far from wrong.

"To what do we owe the honor of this visit?" greeted Wendy, as Willy stepped out of his new Volvo. As far as she was concerned, he could keep his sophisticated clothes and new car. To Wendy, the Tweeds were still rich intruders. If Robin wanted to live over there it was her business.

The Tweeds had a large stable of horses, a beautiful swimming pool, and a full staff of servants. It seemed to Wendy that they had a little *too* much of everything.

"I came to see the Wonder Horse," Willy Tweed said.

"You did? Since when do you like horses?"

"I don't, but I've heard so much about this brute that I decided to come and see for myself," Willy said, and grinned. His crooked grin was hard to resist.

"Harlequin's in the center stall. He loves visitors." There was nothing Wendy liked better than showing off her pet. She decided to give in a little. It wasn't Willy's fault that his father was rich.

Harlequin, hearing them approach, stuck his white head over the door and nickered.

"Wow! He's sure an eye-catcher. A horse show judge can't miss him—and those long lashes—if he were a girl he could bat them at all the boys."

Harlequin, nuzzling for sugar, butted Wendy in the rear. "Stop attacking me, you brute. You've eaten your share already." Wendy slapped him lightly on the nose and stepped out of reach.

"He'd better do more than just bat his eye lashes. I expect him to win. He's got to," she added quietly, "if we're going to make expenses."

Willy studied the girl next to him. Robin had always been the determined one. Now easy going Wendy was following in her younger sister's footsteps. It would seem that the horse really had changed her.

"I'm hoping to take him to the show at Tilly Foster," Wendy said. She leaned over the stall door and watched the horse thoughtfully. "It's a small one and not too far away. It will be a good show for us to start at, but..." She was thinking of expenses. Horse shows, even local ones, cost plenty.

"Who is going to drive the trailer for you?"

"Dad...I guess." Wendy hadn't planned that far.

"I'll take you," Willy volunteered. "I like driving trailers."

"That would be great." If Wendy was surprised at the offer she did not show it. "It's a week from this Saturday."

"I know, and I'll be here in plenty of time to pick you and Harlequin up."

"Thanks a lot. That will be a big help." Wendy walked her guest back to his car. A Volvo looked much better in the stable yard than an Austin Healey, she decided.

"See you."

Before Wendy could answer, Willy's car was down the driveway. She was still recovering from the Tweed charm when Robin steamed into the yard.

"Granny's here, and Mom wants you to come and say hello."

"Darn!" It slipped out unintentionally. Wendy was fond of her grandmother, but she wished she had come an hour later. There was work to be done in the stable.

Granny Babcock was Mrs. Fleming's mother. Since Grandpa's death several years ago, she and Fifi, her miniature poodle, lived in town. Granny didn't come to the country often. She thought it was too much for her. She wasn't so old, but she felt old. "Nobody needs me, anymore," Granny always told her daughter. When Wendy's mother suggested that she should work for a hospital within walking distance of her apartment, her answer was always the same. "I don't want to say I'm going to volunteer and then not feel well enough to do it. What would happen if I promised to help in the Admitting Office of New York Hospital and then get one of my dizzy spells?" That argument always stopped Mom cold. Margaret Fleming knew that most of the spells were caused by boredom, but she realized that if she tried to explain that, Gran would never believe her.

"Hi, Granny!" Wendy found her grandmother seated on one of the straight backed chairs in the library. She was a heavy woman with a pretty face and lovely gray hair.

Fifi was at her feet, guarding her enormous pocket book. "Granny's trunk," Robin called it. It looked like it weighed a ton.

"One of my old lady friends lent me her car and chauffeur for the day, and I decided to pay you all a visit." Granny sounded well pleased with her excursion.

"That's swell," Wendy said. She glanced at her mother. Mom winced as usual when Gran talked about her "old lady friends."

"If she didn't talk so old, she wouldn't feel so old," Mom always said. But how was one going to change Granny Babcock?

"What do you want for your birthday, Wendy?" her grandmother asked. "It's coming up in two weeks." Giving presents was Granny's favorite indoor sport. "Do you have any projects this year?" she inquired.

"Does she ever!" Robin had to put her two cents in.

Wendy gave her sister an annoyed look and to hide her embarrassment concentrated on petting Fifi. "I have a large project, Granny. Perhaps you can help me with it." Suddenly she had an idea. She whispered something to Robin, then disappeared from the room.

"Let's take Fifi for a walk, Gran," Robin suggested. She knew that by the time she got Granny moving, Wendy would have a head start.

"That's a good idea, Robin. Both of us could use a little fresh air."

Robin handed her grandmother her cane, picked her "trunk" up off the floor, and whistled to Fifi. The little city dog loved the country and was already waiting at the door. Gran moved slowly but with determination. If anyone could make her forget that she was an old lady, her grandchildren could.

The procession moved toward the paddock. Fifi frolicked ahead, excitedly sniffing the country smells. Every few strides she'd stop and bark at a squirrel. It had been a long while since she'd been off a leash, and running on green grass was far superior to walking city streets.

Granny moved like a battleship, her progress slow but steady. Fifi was the peppy PT boat darting ahead, and Robin, guiding her grandmother to the paddock, was the destroyer escort.

"What does Wendy want to show me?" Granny sounded more innocent than she really was. "Do you have a new litter of kittens?"

Robin just smiled. She had grown three inches over the winter and now seemed to tower over her grandmother. "You'll see," she said.

Out of the corner of her eye she watched Wendy and Harlequin heading for the paddock. At the rate Granny was walking, Wendy would have time to warm Harley up. Sometimes Granny's slowness was a blessing.

"That's what Wendy wants to show you," said Robin proudly. The leafy maples hindered the view, but Granny could see flashes of her granddaughter sitting very straight on a white-faced chestnut.

When Wendy saw them she circled Harlequin and headed at the post-and-rail jump. They soared over. As they reached the gate she pulled up.

"That was beautiful!" Robin said.

"What a handsome horse, my dear!" Gran told her. Gran didn't know much about riding, but she was fond of animals and devoted to her grandchildren. What she liked most was the blissful expression on Wendy's face.

"I guess your birthday present will be something for the horse this year."

"That would be wonderful, Gran, if you could help me with a few of his expenses. I don't want Harlequin to cost Dad anything."

"I think something could be arranged." Gran was proud of her granddaughter's attitude. "But what happens next month?"

"Perhaps he'll win enough to earn his keep."

That's pure wishful thinking, Robin thought. She knew about horse show economics. At best Harley might earn back his entry fees, but he would never be able to pay for his feed. However, she said nothing. She wasn't going to put a damper on Wendy's plans.

7

Saturday dawned bright and hot. Wendy awoke first and was at the stable by 6 A.M. Willy and the trailer were to arrive at 7:30.

Harlequin had changed Wendy's schedule completely. She no longer slept the mornings away. Now she was up early feeding the horses. Daily, at eight, both girls were in the saddle, and by the time the July heat had started in earnest, Georgetown and Harlequin had been worked and put away.

On four afternoons a week, while Robin and Janie lazed around the Tweeds' pool, Wendy baby sat. She was good with youngsters, and knowing that she was helping to support her horse made up for some of the fun she missed. The moment Harlequin arrived she had given up the idea of a department store job. Baby sitting wasn't as glamorous, but it was easier to fit into the riding schedule.

The chestnut responded well to his deluxe treatment and thrived on the green grass, special feed, and expensive dust free bedding. His coat began to shine, and although no one could call him fat, his bony frame was beginning to fill out.

"It's like the ad on television," Robin said, as she helped stir Harlequin's bucket of beet pulp and non-allergenic grains. "All you need to add is love."

Wendy laughed, but Robin wasn't far from wrong. The old horse tried his best to please, and Wendy had only praise for him. She didn't jump him too much. He didn't need it. But the hours she spent getting him fit showed results. He answered to the touch of her hands and legs and no longer tried to take off with her.

When the Tweed trailer drove into the yard Wendy was putting the last braid in Harlequin's mane. As Tilly Foster did not include a pony division, Georgetown and Snooks were left behind. Today was Harlequin's day.

Robin and Janie had volunteered to be his grooms. But lugging saddles, bridles, buckets, and feed for Harlequin wasn't going to be the same as looking after their own ponies.

Willy was the chauffeur but, like a union member, he specified that driving, and not the care of the horse, was his job. He let the tailgate down and stood with arms folded while Robin and Janie loaded gear into the front partition of the trailer.

"That brother of mine!" spluttered Janie, laden with tack. "He's just too lazy to stir his stumps!"

Willy, hearing the familiar complaint, retorted, "A deal's a deal, girls. I'm skilled labor, you're the hired hands."

"They're not hired hands! They're volunteers, and they're nice enough to help." Wendy bristled at Willy's attitude.

"Keep your shirt on. I was just teasing." To prove it, Willy snapped the lead shank onto Harlequin's halter and started to guide him toward the trailer.

"Here, let me do that." Wendy was afraid that Willy might frighten her horse.

First she checked his leg bandages. Then she carefully walked him into the trailer. Willy closed the tailgate while Wendy saw to it that everything had been loaded. Robin and Janie were in the car, and for the moment a truce was called.

Willy drove carefully. He took the turns slowly, and Harlequin rode quietly.

"You'd hardly know there was a horse in the back," Wendy marveled.

"My superior driving, of course."

At that moment Harlequin kicked out. Thump, went the tailgate.

"Your customer is complaining," Robin said, and laughed.

Willy slowed down and they arrived at Tilly Foster without further excitement.

Harlequin was entered in the junior hunter division which consisted of three classes over the outside course and one in the ring. As the class in the ring was not over jumps, the course worried Wendy.

The public address system was in the process of being hooked up. The local canteen was getting ready to serve food. At the judges' stand, the show secretary was busy making last minute entries.

Wendy was taking Harlequin sight-seeing.. The jumps did not look as difficult as the Tweeds', but the field was rough and hilly. Harlequin was sure to try picking up speed on the home stretch.

Robin, with Janie in tow, watched Wendy show her horse the obstacles. If Harlequin started rolling and Wendy could not hold him, they'd be in trouble.

Robin had an idea. "Hey, Sis," she called, dashing over to Wendy. "I don't think you should take Harlequin over the course."

"Why not?" Wendy sounded belligerent. "That's the reason we came early."

"Sure thing, but you know Harley will jump all the fences. Your only problem will be his speed."

"Yes, but . . ." Then Wendy began to see her point.

"The first time around he'll go slowly and look at his fences. You have three classes on the course. Why take Harlequin around a fourth time?"

Wendy thought a minute. "You're right . . . but what about me? I've got to get a jump under my belt." Horse show nerves are an occupational hazard, but on a new horse they can be doubly bad.

Robin glanced at her sister. Wendy's face looked strained. Why couldn't she be as calm as Harlequin? The old campaigner had been to dozens of shows, and his nerves seemed completely steady.

"You don't need to have a cow about it," Robin said, using her latest favorite expression. "Take a fence, but jump it backwards." She had a good head on her shoulders, especially when it came to horses.

"Which one?"

Robin shrugged. "The chicken coop is as good as any."

By this time other exhibitors were on the course, and horses were jumping in all directions. "Let's get on with it. If you wait any longer, we'll get run over. "Heads up!" called Robin as Wendy circled Harlequin and approached the coop. For a moment the road was clear, and however nervous and tense she felt, Wendy controlled herself. She let Harlequin slip into a smooth slow canter, and he jumped the coop in stride. "That's all you need," Robin called and Wendy nodded. She let out a sigh of relief and, petting her horse, walked back to the trailer.

Willy had parked Harlequin's trailer under a tree where it wasn't too warm. They would have a half hour wait until the first class. There was no point in wearing her horse out.

"How about a doughnut?" Willy asked.

"No thanks," she replied, "but I'll walk over with you. I have to pick up my number."

Now that she had lost weight, Wendy was wearing her mother's good English riding coat and breeches, and her best black riding boots which Granny had given her for her last birthday.

Willy looked at Wendy. In his opinion, a bikini was more becoming on a girl, but he had to admit that she looked pretty sharp.

"You look cool!" he said. "But do you ever wear anything besides breeches or blue jeans?"

"Of course!" Wendy didn't know whether to be flattered or insulted. She decided on the former. "I didn't think you noticed anything but sports cars."

"Oh, sometimes I do," he said casually, and took a huge bite out of his doughnut.

They picked up Harlequin's number and hurried back

to the trailer. Wendy's was the first class and she wanted to get her horse ready. She rubbed off his back, put on the saddle, and gave him a swig of cough medicine before she bridled him. He swallowed most of it but managed to dribble a little down her coat.

"That'll stop the tickle in your throat," she said, wiping the sticky stuff off her front. She didn't want him to cough.

"Class one to the starter, please," the announcer called. Much to her surprise, Willy held her horse as she mounted.

"Want me to give your number to the starter?"

"Please. It's 19."

The first class was to be ridden by juniors and was to be judged entirely on how the horse performed. Wendy jogged Harlequin up and down to limber him up and then stood at the start watching the contestants ahead of her. It was the first round of the day, and the performance left much to be desired. One of the horses stopped at the chicken coop. Another took two strides in the in-and-out, and a third slowed down at the wall. Most of them came home faster than they started.

"Just keep an even feel of Harley's mouth and straighten up a little between fences. He'll do the rest," Robin whispered.

"I'll try," Wendy said, but she did not sound confident. As her number was called she circled Harlequin into the first brush fence. Her nervousness began to leave her, and she concentrated on giving her horse a good ride. Harlequin had a way of setting his own pace. If she didn't upset him, they'd be in business. The seasoned campaigner paid little attention to the brush. Before Wendy realized it they were over and heading for the post-and-rail fence.

Harley had jumped hundreds like it before, and it proved to be no problem. The chicken coop was a breeze, but now came the turn toward home and the stone wall. Wendy could feel the chestnut's stride increasing. For a second she was tempted to shorten her reins. If she did he'd toss his head or, worse, take hold of the bit and start to run. Instead, she straightened her body and talked to him. "Whoa, boy, take it easy, whoa." Harley relaxed and hit the wall just right. The thoroughbred's white legs covered the ground in even strides. When he jumped she felt as if they were flying. Only two more obstacles and they'd be home free. Wendy was so busy enjoying herself that she let Harlequin increase slightly, bringing him a shade under the in of the in-and-out. But Harlequin was clever and covered up for her mistake. The last jump was the white gate, and Harlequin sailed over it.

Robin and the Tweeds standing at the final fence applauded. The judges marked their cards, and the next horse came out on the course.

Wendy pulled up in a daze. She had never felt such a round. She knew without being told that she had just had a terrific go.

A few more horses jumped, the judges signed their cards and then handed them to the ring master.

"You've got it in the bag," Janie told her.

"No one came close to Harlequin!" Willy was sure of that, but Wendy kept her fingers crossed. Exhibitors, spectators, and judges do not always see eye to eye.

"We have the results of Class One, junior working hunters," the announcer called. "First, number 19, Harlequin, ridden by Wendy Fleming."

Wendy did not listen to the rest. She threw her arms

around her horse and hugged him. The thoroughbred looked a little startled, but good-naturedly nuzzled the girl's pockets for sugar.

"Enough of this love making—they're waiting for you at the judges' stand. Don't you want to get your trophy?" Willy said teasingly.

Wendy grinned at him as she jogged over to the stand. A lady presented her with a small silver bowl and pinned a blue ribbon on the chestnut's brow.

"Thank you so much!" Wendy said happily and walked her wonder horse back to the trailer.

She didn't bother to hold onto the reins. She knew Harlequin would follow her. Sugar might be bad for his teeth, and it might make him nip, but it certainly was the way to his heart. If she didn't win another ribbon all day, her summer was made.

But she kept on winning. She won in the hack class in the ring where Harlequin was judged on way of moving and manners, and also in the second working hunter class. Only the stake was yet to come.

In each division at a horse show the stake is the money class. At Tilly Foster the entry fee was ten dollars, but the winner would receive fifty dollars. If Wendy could only win she would make her expenses for the day.

"You can do it!" Robin told her as Wendy saddled Harlequin for their final class. "Remember," she said, "trophies are great, but cash is better."

Wendy had to smile. When it came to money, Robin was a sharpy.

The stake was Harlequin's third time over the course. As Robin had predicted, he moved faster. Wendy knew, however, that if the pace is even, judges don't object to speed in this class. She managed to put Harlequin in the groove, and he responded with a spectacular jumping round.

They made a clean sweep. The championship was theirs, and so was the fifty dollar prize.

After the champ was given a much needed washing down and loaded into the trailer, the Flemings and Tweeds rode home in contented silence. Wendy was too excited to talk much. Robin and Janie had cheered themselves hoarse, and Willy was concentrating on his driving. A champ needed the smoothest ride possible.

"I've never never had a day like this," said Wendy finally. "I want to thank all of you . . . for everything." There was a slight catch in her throat.

"No speeches, please!" Willy was in his element. "We'll have lots more shows, and if the small fry behave, we'll let them bring their ponies."

8

Janie, Willie, and Robin did the victory dinner justice. Wendy, still on cloud nine, was too excited to eat much. But Robin, patting her flat stomach, groaned and said, "I'm stuffed. I can't eat another bite of lemon meringue pie."

Mom and Dad listened quietly while the girls and Willy regaled them with the exciting events of the day. Mr. Fleming was delighted that Wendy, as well as Robin, now had a good horse.

"I'll help with the dishes, Mom," Wendy volunteered after saying goodnight to Willy and his sister. "Small fry can't keep her eyes open. You'd think *she'd* ridden all day."

"There is nothing more tiring than spectating," Margaret Fleming said, understandingly. "You'd better go to bed, dear."

"What about the dishes?"

"Wendy and I are quite capable of doing them."

Robin was not the kind to shirk a job but bed sounded mighty good. "I know what!" she said, brightening considerably. "Wendy can sleep late tomorrow. I'll feed the horses."

Wendy gave her sister an affectionate shove toward the stairs. "That would be great!" she said. "I'll do the same for you and Georgetown someday."

As the excitement began to wear off, Wendy realized how bone tired she was. She was dying to turn in, but she was reluctant to sleep yet.

"Mom . . ." she began hesitatingly, "I'd like to talk to you about Harlequin. Muriel is going to hear that Harlequin was champion today and she might decide that she was foolish to lend him to me." Wendy suddenly found that she had a hard time holding back her tears. She couldn't, she just couldn't give Harley up.

Mrs. Fleming listened quietly, knowing how much Harlequin meant to Wendy.

"If only, if only . . ."

"We could buy him." Her mother finished the sentence. Margaret Fleming stared at the now empty coffee cup. She too was sure that as soon as Muriel's folks heard about Wendy's and Harlequin's success, they would not be satisfied with the present arrangement. If George could only help. She shook her head. Her husband had enough problems without her involving him in this one.

"I'm the rich member of the family," Robin piped up. Too tired to sleep, she had wandered down the back stairs. Minus slippers, Robin had made so little noise that Mrs. Fleming and Wendy had not heard her. "My savings bank is full of the money Janie's dad paid me for Snooks last year. She perched herself on the kitchen table and made Wendy a proposition. "I'll lend you the cash to buy Harlequin, and some day you can repay me—with interest, of course." She wasn't sure how interest worked, but it sounded very businesslike.

Wendy thought about it. Could Robin help her out? For a moment she toyed with the idea.

"No," she said finally. "How could I ever repay you? And what's more, Dad would never permit it." Wendy looked at her mother who nodded in agreement.

"I may have a thought, girls," Mom said encouragingly. "Let me sleep on it."

Wendy watched her mother as she walked toward the library. If anyone could solve the problem, she could, Wendy thought, and felt better already.

Mrs. Fleming rose early the following morning and bustled about keeping herself busy until she could make her important call. But long before that time Applebee Farm's phone rang.

"This is Grace Alexander," said the voice at the other end of the line. "I want to congratulate you on how well Wendy and Harlequin did at Tilly Foster."

Mrs. Fleming was a little startled at how quickly the Alexanders had reacted. "How very kind of you," she answered, hoping that her voice did not sound as panicky as she felt.

After a few more pleasantries Mrs. Alexander came to the point. "Muriel hasn't heard about the horse show yet." She sounded like a conspirator. "But when she does, I am sure she'll want to ride the horse herself."

Margaret Fleming was silent.

"Wendy wouldn't like that, would she?"

Mrs. Fleming did not answer. If she had she might have said something she would have later regretted.

"I'm not particularly anxious to have Harlequin back. We promised Muriel a horse to make school more palatable." Mrs. Alexander mentioned the name of a stylish Virginia boarding school. "But Harlequin didn't help. Muriel couldn't adjust to school discipline and after three months she was suspended for smoking marihuana." The woman's voice sounded distraught. "First she wanted a horse, now she wants a car. What will she want next? Muriel's extravagance is driving us into debt. I don't see how she can go around looking as if we never spent a penny on her." The long pent-up words spilled out. "We'll have to sell Harlequin to pay for the Austin Healey."

"He's well worth it, but . . ." Margaret Fleming, trying to sound businesslike, was not about to say, you're not the only one with money problems. Instead, in a controlled voice, she continued, "Give me a couple of days and I'll see what I can do." She hung up. For a long time she stared at the phone. Finally she dialed New York.

Wendy was in no hurry to get up. Robin was taking care of Harlequin, and she could revel in the luxury of staying in bed and thinking over the events of yesterday. Harley had won. He had won every class and the championship. Even in the days of her pony, Mr. Darling, she had never done as well. Robin had never done as well. Muriel Alexander had never even come close. With Bitsy for company at her side, she day dreamed of horse shows to come, the trophies she and Harley would win, and the prize money that would more than pay for his expenses.

When she finally came downstairs, the house was empty.

Wendy fixed herself some breakfast and curled up on the library sofa. Magazine in hand she planned to spend a few lazy hours.

By lunch time she began to wonder where everybody was. She hurried down to the barn, but the horses were out at pasture and all appeared happy. Harlequin, none the worse for yesterday, was busily grazing. Robin and Mom were nowhere in sight. Perhaps they had gone marketing.

Wendy made herself a sandwich and was about to take Bitsy for a walk when she heard a car coming up the drive. That must be her mother and sister, she thought. Why did they walk out and not even tell her where they were going?

However, it was a strange car, not their mile-weary station wagon, that pulled up at the door. Wendy did a double take. It was Granny, and she was driving a snappy, blue coupe.

"Granny, I didn't know you could drive!"

"Child, I'm a very good driver," Granny said, as she kissed her affectionately. "When I was in the Motor Corps during World War I, I thought nothing of driving for hours, or even changing a tire. They were always blowing out in those days," she said, and smiled. "I looked pretty sporty in my long skirt and driving goggles, but . . . old ladies don't belong behind the wheel. Their reactions aren't fast enough."

"I had to come here on business," she continued, noticing Wendy's questioning look. "I can't afford a chauffeur, so I rented this car, and here I am." Granny then walked briskly into the house.

Wendy had not seen her grandmother move so fast in years.

"Where is your mother?"

"I don't know. She's been out for hours."

Granny smiled. "Never mind. My business is with you."

"With me?" The puzzle was deepening. What could her grandmother want?

Granny made herself and Fifi comfortable in the library. "Your mother is always telling me that I lack interests," she began. "And that I'd be much happier if I did something other than play bridge and talk on the telephone."

Wendy smiled. She could almost hear Mom lecturing Granny.

"Margaret may be right," her grandmother continued. "But since your Grandfather died there has been nothing I've wanted to do. Now, I think I have found something of interest." Granny looked more pleased than Wendy ever remembered. "But I'll need your help."

Her help? How could she help? Did she want her company at that resort hotel at the Cape? It had been deadly last year. How could she go away now that she had Harlequin. These thoughts raced through her mind. Hesitatingly, she said, "Of course, Gran. I'd love to help you." To hide her confusion she got up and fetched Fifi some water.

Gran had put Wendy to the test and she had come through well. Mrs. Babcock patted her dog and continued briskly. "I want to buy a horse." She let the bombshell sink in.

"You want to buy a horse? What would you do with it?"

"I want to buy Harlequin!"

Wendy ran over to her grandmother and gave her a

big hug. When she found her voice she asked excitedly, "You want to buy him for *me?*"

"I said no such thing, young lady." Granny looked very wise. "I want to be a horse owner. Of course, I shall need you to ride him for me and to teach me all about show horses." Almost to herself she added, "I wish my father could see me now. He was a great horseman and he was always disappointed that none of his children shared his interest."

Wendy, not knowing whether to laugh or cry, proceeded to dance a jig around the room.

9

"We thought you'd never get home," Gran said, obviously delighted to see her daughter. "Wendy and I have so much to tell you."

Mom laughed. "You seem to have manged very well without me," she said. She took one look at the blissful pair and knew that Gran's mission had been successful. Her mother already seemed different. She was needed now and that was what Gran had always wanted.

"I'll be so busy with Harlequin," said Granny, studying the small notebook she carried in her purse, "that I will have to call New York. They'll just have to do without me for a day or so."

"Then you'll stay?" Mom was delighted.

"That will be the best arrangement, I think," Granny said, making it sound as if it were an everyday occurrence. She had not spent a night at the farm in years. The stairs were too hard on her, she had always complained, and so was a room without air conditioning.

Mrs. Babcock handed Wendy the car keys and with utmost nonchalance said, "Would you fetch my overnight bag, dear?"

Wendy beamed at her mother, and when Mom was sure that no one was looking, she gave her daughter Mr. Churchill's old "V" for victory sign. Her plan was working far better than she could ever have imagined.

Mrs. Fleming brought some coffee, coke, and cookies into the library. Behind her trailed Bitsy and Fifi. At the first sign of food the dogs were always on hand.

While Wendy, her mother, and Granny nibbled the brownies and discussed Harlequin, a car drove into the Flemings' driveway.

"That must be Mrs. Alexander. I asked her to come over and see me. Wen, dear, let her in please," Granny Babcock said. She was plainly in her element.

"What's she doing here?" Wendy's question was directed at her mother, but Granny answered.

"There's more to buying a horse than saying yes, over the telephone. Grace Alexander is here so that we can finalize the deal. Now snap to it, young lady, and open the door." It was clear that Granny was enjoying herself thoroughly.

The dowdy woman who followed Wendy into the library bore little resemblance to Muriel. She was small and plump. At the moment she appeared thoroughly ill at ease. In one hand she clutched a shiny leather pocket book, in the other, she hung onto a half smoked cigaret.

After the introductions had been made and Grace Alexander was seated, Granny took over.

"Mrs. Alexander and I have business to discuss." She looked at her daughter and granddaughter.

Wendy, taken by surprise, was about to say something, but her mother took her by the arm. "We're not wanted, Wen," she said, with a smile. "Granny's in command."

Granny winked, then turning to Mrs. Alexander she started the conference. "I know we're both anxious to complete the sale of Harlequin."

Mrs. Alexander nodded and nervously lit another cigaret. Now it was Mrs. Babcock's turn to hesitate. Saying she'd buy the horse had been one thing, but paying several thousand dollars was another. She settled herself in the comfortable chair. After studying Mrs. Alexander a moment, she inquired casually, "Have you bought the car for Muriel?"

"Oh, yes. She's been driving it for a week and she's been stopped twice already."

"Speeding?" Granny asked.

Mrs. Alexander nodded unhappily. "Muriel is so impetuous. I'm scared to death for her. Perhaps it was all a big mistake. She could get into far less trouble with a horse than in a high powered car."

The conversation was not going the way Granny had planned. She now tried another tack. "How are you paying for the car?"

"On the installment plan, of course." Grace Alexander dropped the stub of her cigaret in the ash tray and immediately lit another. "We couldn't possibly afford it in one lump sum."

"And neither can I." Granny thought she could not have planned it better. "I would like to pay for Harlequin the same way you are paying for the car."

Grace Alexander fidgeted nervously with her finger-nails. "That would be all right, I guess," she finally said. "Providing, of course, that it covers the car payments."

"Naturally." Granny was relieved that it had gone over so well. "How much are your monthly installments?" She dug into her alligator carryall, pulled her check book out of the bottomless pit and proceeded to write.

Both women were greatly relieved. Grace Alexander had worried that the Flemings and Mrs. Babcock might change their minds, and Granny had not been at all sure that the Alexanders would be willing to accept her method of payment.

As they shook hands, Grace Alexander said politely, "I do hope your granddaughter will enjoy Harlequin. If only I could be sure that the car will satisfy Muriel," she added. "We're trying so hard to make her happy and all she does is act as if we were her worst enemies, and threaten to run away. We don't know what to do any-more."

By the end of the second day Granny knew everything about the stable. Fifi too had become a country dog. She and Bitsy spent hours craftily watching moles dig endless subterranean tunnels. Squirrel-chasing was their second choice. The most fun, however, was guarding the numer-ous woodchuck holes.

Gran's notebook worked overtime. Harlequin was to be outfitted. Mrs. Babcock was all for having a well dressed horse. Catalogue in hand Wendy and her grandmother studied charts and measured their flag bearer. "It says, if a horse is 15.2 hands high, he needs a 72 inch blanket."

Wendy, sucking her pencil, looked at Harlequin questioningly. "What do you think, Gran?"

Comfortably seated on the roomy mounting block, Mrs. Babcock supervised, "I'm a fine one to ask," she said, and burst out laughing. "You're supposed to be the expert. What do I know about horse overcoats?"

"Well, 72 inches it is then. Dad always says this company is reasonable and the most reliable," Wendy said, and tapped the catalogue.

"Harley will need a sheet and blanket," she continued as she leafed through the pages with obvious pleasure.

"Is that all?" Gran sounded disappointed.

"Those are the essentials, but if you feel flush, a show horse can use a cooler, and a rain and fly sheet. But haven't you spent enough money already?" Her family's financial problems had made Wendy money conscious.

"Let's be extravagant," Gran said. She was like a kid with a new toy.

"We'll get green sheets with yellow bindings. Those were always our stable colors." Wendy remembered when Applebee Farm's horses were well turned out.

They added a new halter complete with nameplate, several buckets, rub rags, and brushes. And to carry the works Granny ordered Harlequin a tack trunk.

"You're sure that your saddle and Harlequin's bridle are okay?" Her daughter's trousseau had been her last big shopping spree, and she was thoroughly enjoying her present splurge.

"You're the last of the red-hot spenders, Gran!" Wendy exclaimed.

"Hardly . . ." Mrs. Babcock hesitated. "But this is much

more fun than buying clothes for my fat self." Arm in arm the two walked back to the house.

By the third day Granny had to return to town. She had already broken several lunch and dental appointments. Monday was her Play of the Month Club. She did not want to miss that.

"If you insist on driving to town on Sunday, I think you should leave in the early afternoon," Mom said. She did not like the idea of Granny bucking the weekend traffic.

"Whatever you say," Granny answered. She was thoroughly enjoying the Flemings' Sunday luncheon. Mom had prepared a feast, and Dad, not to be outdone, had produced one of his last bottles of French wine.

"I'll leave directly after we have eaten." Margaret's trying to slow her down amused her, for her daughter had always been the one who had wanted her to do more.

"I don't like to see you go," Margaret Fleming said. She put her hand affectionately over her mother's.

"I second that motion!" Dad said. He also was delighted with the "new Granny." Picking up his glass he declared, "I'd like to propose a toast to Harlequin and his owner!"

Granny beamed. Everyone, even Robin, sipped the wine, although the latter made a terrible face and needed a water chaser.

"What's the matter with milk?" she asked obstinately. "Wine is terrible stuff!" But a superior look from Wendy was all she got for her trouble.

"To my jockey," Mrs. Babcock returned the compliment. "May the three of us have a successful season."

"Thanks for all your help," Wendy added to the happiness of the moment... and then the door bell rang.

"Answer it, please, Rob. Tell whoever it is that we're

at lunch," Margaret Fleming said. She did not want to interrupt this family occasion.

As Robin grudgingly headed for the door Granny could not resist teasing her daughter. "If you're not careful, Maggie" (it wasn't often that Granny Babcock called her daughter by her long-forgotten nickname), "I might turn into the Granny 'who came to dinner.'"

"That would be wonderful!" responded her daughter. "Did you notice that we had the stairs especially rebuilt for you? They are so much easier to climb now."

George Fleming kept a straight face, but Wendy laughed out loud. "Stop teasing the owner of the horse I love," she said with mock severity. "Granny went up the stairs three times yesterday." But the good-natured bantering stopped short as Robin returned to the table.

"What is it, dear?" her mother asked, alarmed at the look on Robin's face.

Robin, attempting composure, answered, "It's just . . . it's Muriel Alexander. She wants Harlequin back."

"She *what?*" Wendy asked. She couldn't believe that she had heard her sister correctly. "She can't have him! We've bought him!" And with that she dashed to the door.

In a moment George Fleming followed, but Muriel pushed past them and flounced into the dining room.

"I want my horse! What have you done with him?" screamed the hysterical girl. Her long hair was dishevelled, her eyes smeared and red from crying.

"We haven't done anything with him. Sit down, my dear," Mrs. Fleming said with concern in her voice.

"Where is he? Where is he?" demanded Muriel, as if she expected to find him in the dining room.

"In the stable of course," Wendy interrupted, not taking her eyes off Muriel.

What had happened to Muriel, she wondered. If possible, she looked even more unkempt than the last time Wendy had seen her. Her shirt and jeans were riddled with holes. A thong was missing from one of her sandals, and her feet, ingrained with dirt, looked sorely in need of attention.

Mrs. Fleming gave Wendy her "don't interfere" look and continued. "You have your car, Muriel. What seems to be the trouble?"

"I want my horse, I want him. Mother had no right to sell him." She buried her face in her hands and sobbed uncontrollably. "I want both." And between loud sobs she mumbled, "I don't know what I want. I'm just so miserable."

Mrs. Fleming put her arms around the overwrought girl. "Now Muriel," she said kindly, "you've got to make some sense."

But Muriel was in no mood to make sense. She shook herself free and dashed over to George Fleming. "You've got to help me," she insisted. "There's been a terrible mistake." With tears streaming down her face, she grabbed his coat and hung onto it.

George Fleming disentangled himself and in his most patient voice said, "Muriel, the horse doesn't belong to you anymore. Your mother sold him to us so that she could buy you a car. She thought that was what you wanted."

"I want both! I want both!" she cried. She then picked up the nearest ash tray and hurled it at the wall.

"That's quite enough, young lady." George Fleming's

voice had taken on a new note. "You can't act like that in this house." He took her by the arm and escorted her to the door.

For a moment the family was speechless. "What a nerve!" Robin was the first to find her voice.

"She's all mixed up," Wendy said, visibly shaken by the scene.

"If I were her mother, I'd worry about that child. She's more than mixed up, she's sick," said Mrs. Fleming.

"Her mother does worry," Mrs. Babcock replied quietly. "It's just that the poor woman doesn't know which way to turn."

"Then there's going to be trouble," Mrs. Fleming stated flatly.

"Granny . . ." Wendy hesitated, her face clouded, "do you think you should delay your shopping spree?"

"Nonsense, child! A Babcock doesn't worry about the likes of Muriel Alexander. I bought the horse legally and in good faith. No one is going to take him away from me."

The old lady had backbone, and for the moment Wendy felt better . . . but not for long.

10

"The days of horse thieves are over, Wen." George Fleming kidded his daughter as he left for the office the following day. But he did not count on the persistence of Muriel Alexander.

Not a day passed without one or more phone calls from Muriel, and as the weeks progressed she became more and more vituperative.

The Flemings didn't know that Muriel and her mother had engaged in a violent battle at soon as the unhappy girl learned of the sale of her horse. They fought about many things—Muriel's appearance, the company she kept, her smoking habits. But the battle about Harlequin was the worst yet. Muriel may have suggested sparing her parents the expense of supporting Harlequin while she was talking them into buying her a car, but she had not been ready to have her champion sold.

However hard the Alexanders tried to please their daughter they failed, and Muriel made sure that her parents knew how much they failed.

"I want my horse back," Muriel had screamed at Mrs. Fleming in a final telephone onslaught. "If you won't let me have him, I'll come and take him. You wait and see."

"If this keeps up, leave the receiver off the hook," Mr. Fleming told his wife, but Mrs. Fleming could not do that indefinitely. Soon thereafter Applebee Farm's phone was changed to an unlisted number, and Muriel no longer bothered them.

That ended the affair as far as the grownups were concerned. Granny Babcock jokingly offered to hire a watchman. However, even she did not take seriously the threat to Harlequin's safety.

Wendy, though usually easygoing, believed differently. Once she decided to take action it was not difficult for her to influence Robin. Janie caught the spirit of the affair also, and her brother Willy, always ready for an adventure, made a game of it.

"Wendy Fleming wants a council of war at five today," Janie informed him. A foreign minister advising his head of state of an impending international conference could not have taken his mission more seriously. "Can we count on you?" she asked.

"Sure thing!" he responded. The thought of playing James Bond intrigued him a bit. "Shall I bring my gun?"

"*Very* funny!" Why couldn't her brother ever take anything seriously?

But at five o'clock when Wendy called the meeting to order in Applebee Farm's tack room, Willy was present and accounted for.

"Thanks for coming so promptly. It's an emergency, you know," Wendy said. She laughed nervously. "I hope I'm not letting my imagination get the better of me. But now that Muriel can't pester us by phone, I'm afraid she'll find another way of getting even."

"For selling a horse and getting well paid for it? What a fink!" Robin retorted.

"There's nothing wrong with buying on the installment plan. Everybody does it," said Wendy defensively.

"Nothing," Willy agreed. "I don't really see what all the fuss is about. Muriel can't take Harlequin without actually stealing him. And she's certainly not going to do that. Let's adjourn the meeting and go swimming." He was beginning to lose interest in this horse opera.

"That's what you think!" exclaimed Wendy. "Come look at the yard!" Plain for everyone to see, next to Harlequin's stall were fresh car tracks. "Robin and I raked the gravel yesterday. Somebody must have been here last night."

Willy looked thoughtful. "It shouldn't be hard to identify the car from the tire imprints."

"I'm willing to bet they belong to an Austin Healey," remarked Wendy. "Who else would come here at night?"

"You've got a point," Willy admitted. Deep in thought he strode back and forth in front of Harlequin's stall. The white-faced chestnut eyed him curiously. When he saw no sugar forthcoming he stamped his foot impatiently. Turning his back on his uncooperative visitors, he decided to concentrate on his salt lick.

Robin, watching the horse, burst out laughing. "I do believe Harlequin feels neglected. Come here, Harley."

She rubbed his ears. Don't you know," she told him, "we're here because of your welfare?"

Willy scowled at the interruption. "I have a plan."

"Shoot!" said Wendy.

"We will have to guard Harlequin," he announced importantly.

"How?" she asked.

"It's simple." Will was enjoying being center stage. He parked himself on the mounting block. "We will take turns watching Harlequin at night. No one is going to walk off with him in broad daylight."

"But where will we sleep?" Janie asked doubtfully.

"In the tack room. It shouldn't be too bad with a sleeping bag."

"All alone?" Thirteen-year-old Janie was thinking less and less of her brother's brainstorm.

"No Janie, not you. I couldn't be that mean to my baby sister." Janie thumbed her nose at him.

"We'll divide the guard into three watches. You and Robin take one night together. I'll take the next, and Wendy can take the third. That way each of us will only have to do it twice a week."

"As soon as Muriel gets wind of our plan, she'll know she's licked," Wendy said, feeling reassured by Will Tweed's idea.

"My turn tonight," Willy volunteered. "I'll go home now, and dig out my equipment. I'll be back as soon as dinner is over."

Willy returned, complete with sleeping bag, flashlight, and transistor radio. He arranged his gear and before turning in, patrolled the stable area. While he was checking the horses' water he heard footsteps. Will slid back into the shadows and held his breath. As the footsteps kept coming closer the flesh on the back of his neck tingled.

"Who's there?" he yelled in his most sentry-like manner, but his voice cracked a little.

"Don't scare me like that!" Wendy whispered. "I nearly dropped the chocolate cake."

"I really thought you were a prowler," he said, hiding his relief. "You're not supposed to be roaming around at this hour."

"Don't you like chocolate cake?" Wendy had expected a better welcome.

"Sure, I do. It's just that you startled me. Where would you like to sit?"

"The mounting block will do."

Willy fetched his radio, and to the accompaniment of the "Supremes" they downed two generous slices of Betty Crocker's best.

Willy sighed contentedly. He put his arm around Wendy and hummed along with the group. Wendy shut her eyes and snuggled closer. Boarding school was never like this.

The night was warm. Near them a restless horse stamped in his stall. High above, stars shimmered while the waning moon cast grotesque shadows on the earth below.

If only this mounting block was softer, thought Willy. He kissed the tip of Wendy's nose.

"I'd better be getting back," Wendy said. "They'll begin to worry about me at the house." She hated to leave.

The next night was Wendy's turn to sleep guard. But until she tried it she did not realize that staying alone in the stable could be so scary. She discovered that normal stable noises and flitting shadows which had seemed romantic the night before now took on an eerie quality.

Flashlight in hand she forced herself to patrol the yard and check each stall. When all the horses were accounted for she felt better.

You've read too many mystery stories, she scolded herself as she slid way down into her sleeping bag. Stop overworking your imagination and get some rest. But sleep would not come until the early dawn cast a friendlier light on Applebee Farm's stable yard.

At breakfast the next morning Wendy was red eyed and grumpy, but she didn't complain. She did not want to discourage Janie and Robin.

But as the days passed, they all became grumpy. A sleeping bag was fun on a camping trip, but in the tack room it soon became tedious.

Willy would have welcomed some excitement, but the girls were more than glad that there was none.

"It's a pest," Robin and Janie finally decided.

"I don't think it's necessary," was Willy's opinion, and soon even Wendy began to have her doubts.

"How long are you planning to keep this up?" Will's father asked Wendy during the second week of "Detectives Incorporated."

"Until after the Long Island shows." Wendy hoped she sounded more positive than she felt.

"In mid-September? That's over a month off!"

Wendy nodded. "I figure that Muriel, like the rest of us, will be going back to school—that is, if any school will take her. Then all our troubles will be over."

"What troubles? All you have found were one set of car

tracks and you are not even sure that they were Muriel's."
Will's father was not convinced.

"I'm positive she still wants Harlequin back and she'll stop at nothing!" said Wendy defensively.

"If you really feel that way, send the horse over to us. You kids have lost enough sleep already. Our groom lives over the stable. Harlequin will be safe there."

"That would be wonderful, but..." Should she accept Mr. Tweed's hospitality?

Will's father studied Wendy, then he said, "You can take care of the horse yourself and bring your own feed if you like."

"Oh, yes, that would be perfect!" Wendy answered, delighted with the suggestion.

And so Harlequin joined Snooks in the Tweeds' palatial stable.

With Harlequin safe and with a little nudging from Willy, Wendy began to understand what had been bugging Muriel. She had tired of Harlequin and had wanted a car, but she had not counted on her mother making a quick sale.

"I think Mrs. Alexander jumped the gun," she confided to Willy. "Perhaps I should let Muriel come over occasionally and ride Harley." It was easy to be magnanimous when the danger had passed and Harlequin was guarded by Jarvis in the Tweed stable.

The girls rode daily. Mostly they worked in the field schooling themselves and their horses. Occasionally they hacked cross-country, and on these jaunts Will accompanied them. According to Willy an outing on horseback was sport, but doing exercises and working on the finer points of riding was sissy stuff.

Granny and the four youngsters attended several local shows and came home loaded with ribbons. While Harlequin repeated his Tilly Foster record and remained the champion, Robin aboard Georgetown and Janie on Snooks also won their share.

Willy was still their chauffeur. Gran arrived later in the morning and always brought lunch. The girls were none too hungry while they were riding, but Granny's fried chicken and brownies were hard to resist.

Gran Babcock loved every minute of it. After each show she collected Harlequin's trophies and took them to town. "To show my old lady friends," she said with a smile. But the next time she came up to the country she always returned them to Wendy. When her granddaughter protested that owners, not riders, always kept the trophies, Granny demurred. "Horse show cups belong in the country. I don't have room for them in my New York apartment."

August flew by, and the following week was the great Piping Rock Horse Show on Long Island. Granny decided to make a party of it. She wrote for rooms at a nearby motel and invited Janie and Will to stay with her and the Flemings. Jarvis was to bring the horses, and all of them were looking forward to a three-day adventure.

Harlequin and the ponies were to ship out early, and the whole day before was to be spent getting them ready.

"This is more work than packing for school," said Wendy, busily filling Harlequin's new trunk.

"You'd think he was a movie star, not a white-faced plug," Willy teased.

"Some plug! I'll take one like him any day." Robin's voice held a note of envy.

The work seemed endless, but by six-thirty that night they finally finished. "Time to quit!" Jarvis announced. "You'd better get home, eat supper, pack your bag, and get a good night's sleep. I wish I could do the same," he grumbled to himself.

"Why can't you?" they asked in unison.

"The mother of a friend of mine died yesterday. I have to go to the wake, and I'll probably get home good and late."

"Do you think Will or I should watch Harley?" Wendy asked.

"No, Miss. No one would dare come into Mr. Tweed's place!" He was convinced of that. Smiling, he added, "To ride well, you have to get your sleep."

"And I'm not about to spend any more nights in a stable. I've had quite enough of that," Will declared.

Wendy was the last to leave. She gave her shiny horse a final pat. "Now, Harlequin," she warned him, "sleep well but don't get peat moss all over your beautiful white face and legs. No time for cleaning tomorrow."

In the early hours of the next morning Jarvis rushed into Will Tweed's bedroom. "Master Will, Master Will, wake up!" he shouted. He shook the boy, trying frantically to rouse him.

"Whatsa matter? What is it?" Willy came to slowly. He rolled over and looked at his watch. Then he sat straight up in bed. "What's the idea?" he demanded sleepily. "It's only three o'clock. Bad enough that I have to get up at five."

Grabbing Willy's shoulder roughly, the groom insisted, "You've got to get up! Harlequin's gone!"

"Harlequin's *what?*" Willy was wide awake now.

"He's gone, vanished, disappeared!" the groom spoke rapidly. "I came home a little after one and checked the horses as I always do. Harlequin's door was wide open. . . ."

"Could Wendy not have shut it properly? She was the last to leave."

"I doubt it." The horseman mopped his face. "I've spent the last two hours searching the neighborhood."

"Any hoofprints?"

"No."

"Car tracks?"

"No." He shook his head. "The ground's so dry you couldn't trail an elephant."

"We'd better tell Wendy's father and call the police." Willy pulled his pants on, and stuck his feet into the nearest shoes. With his shirttails flapping, he hurried down the stairs after Jarvis. As he hopped in the car the groom gunned it down the drive and headed for Applebee Farm.

George Fleming was easier to rouse than Will had been, and in short order the three were conferring in the library.

"Don't wake the girls," Mr. Fleming counseled. "They'll know soon enough." He listened to Jarvis' story, hesitated a moment, and picked up the phone. By now it was four A.M. The phone rang several times before it was answered.

"Mrs. Alexander?" George Fleming asked.

"Yes, who is this?" mumbled a sleepy voice.

"Is Muriel there?"

"Why do you ask?"

"This is George Fleming, Mrs. Alexander. Harlequin's gone! Where's Muriel?"

"In her room, I hope! I'll go and see. Hold on."

A long three minutes passed. "Muriel's bed hasn't been

slept in," sobbed the woman at the other end of the line. "I told her to forget about that horse. What has she done now? What are *you* going to do?" she asked fearfully. "You won't call the police?"

"I have no choice."

"I suppose not, but please help me find my child." And, as if she had been expecting this awful moment, Grace Alexander hung up the phone.

Convincing the police was another matter. "Don't kid me," said the officer on night duty. "Kids steal most anything, but not a horse. That's too big."

"I'm dead serious." Annoyance crept into Mr. Fleming's voice. "Better send out an alarm for a sixteen-year-old named Muriel Alexander. If you find her, you will find the horse."

Mr. Fleming had just finished all the particulars when it was time for the rest of the family to wake up. For Wendy climbing out of bed at 5 A.M. was routine on a horse show morning. "What's going on?" she demanded, as she came into the library. She was clad only in pajamas, her hair was done up in rollers, and her feet were bare. Seeing Willy, she beat a hasty retreat but returned pronto wearing a dressing gown. "What's wrong?" she asked anxiously.

There was no way to soften the blow. Mr. Fleming put his arm around his big daughter. "Harlequin's been stolen," he said gently. "Muriel Alexander has disappeared, and the police have been alerted. We should get a report in a couple of hours."

"I knew something terrible like this would happen!" She buried her head in his shoulder and sobbed uncontrollably. "It was all just too wonderful to last!"

11

Earlier that same evening, Muriel Alexander had failed to hide her impatience. "Step on it, Toby, we haven't got all night." She snuggled up to her boy friend, but for once Toby would happily have done without her.

Terrence Van Horn III was worried. "Are you sure you want to do this? It sounds like a crazy idea." He was all for a midnight lark, but this just didn't sound right. "Why pick up a horse in the middle of the night? What's the matter with tomorrow morning?"

"You wouldn't understand." Lately Muriel had become expert at putting him in his place.

"No, I don't understand!" Toby smoothed down the back of his new double-breasted blazer. He didn't want to crumple it unnecessarily. If he had known what was in store tonight, he would have worn his oldest clothes.

"In fact I don't understand *you* anymore," Toby raised

his voice for emphasis. "I don't understand the way you look, the way you dress, or the way you've acted lately." He was used to his girls in the latest mod fads, but not looking like perfect slobs.

What had happened to Muriel? She used to be fun, good to look at and game to do anything. All the fellows envied him and whistled when he mentioned her name. Now she looked terrible and she was always sore at someone. At this moment he would have been just as happy if he had never become involved with her or her crazy horse scheme.

Their headlights picked up the high hedges bordering the narrow country road.

"We'll be at the Tweeds' gate soon," Toby said. He shifted gears. The Austin Healey, not used to pulling a trailer, groaned loudly.

"Here's the front gate," whispered Muriel. "Another fifty yards and we'll be at the stable entrance."

"Are you sure you want to go in? We could pick up Harlequin tomorrow."

"Quite sure. He's my horse and I can fetch him when I please."

Muriel was becoming more and more difficult to understand, thought Toby. He shook his head. Women are impossible he decided, especially Muriel.

"Here it is," whispered the girl. They made a right turn and drove up the winding road to the stable.

"Will their groom help us?" inquired Toby naively, as he pulled into the stable yard. "I've never loaded a horse in the dark."

Muriel hesitated only a moment, then said coolly, "If he's here, I'm sure he will." But she knew better. "Dim your lights," she commanded. "We don't want to wake the dogs."

For the sixth night in a row, Muriel had driven over to the Tweeds, concealed her car at the bottom of the lane and walked toward the stable. Finally, tonight Jarvis had obliged. She hardly managed to step into the shadows before the groom's old Ford bumped down the back drive. Sitting up very straight, in his Sunday suit, his white hair brushed and plastered down, Jarvis was off to something special. Muriel figured, correctly, that he would be gone for the evening.

The yard was dark and silent. Ahead of them loomed the gray outline of the stone stable. On either side fell weird shadows made by post-and-rail fences, to the left the white mounting block was barely visible. On the right, the watering trough disappeared into the darkness.

"Why can't we turn the lights on?" complained Toby, groping his way to the stable entrance. "We're not intruders—or are we?" He was getting suspicious.

"Of course we're not!" Muriel told him, almost convincing herself. "But we don't want to wake up the whole place." She pulled back the stable door. Holding a pencil flashlight, Muriel led the way. The cork brick of the handsomely built stable muffled their footsteps. All they could hear was the rustle of sleeping animals.

Which one was Harlequin's stall? Muriel shone the light into each loose box, startling the drowsing animals. At the fourth door she stopped. She took a second look, then pulling back the latch, she walked in.

Harlequin jumped and laid back his ears. He waited for the intruder's next move.

"It's me, you dumb brute. You don't have to be afraid of me."

But the horse was not convinced. If he remembered her voice it was not associated with anything pleasant.

"Just as I thought," Muriel murmured as she noticed the braided mane. "We're just in time."

She found his new head collar hanging on the stall door, pulled it over his head and clipped on a lead shank.

"Toby, give me a hand," she ordered as she tried to pull the unwilling animal out of his stall.

"You lead him. I'll get behind." She took another lead shank that she found, and smacked the unwilling horse. Surprised at this rough treatment, Harlequin lunged out of his stall, nearly knocking Toby down.

"Watch it!" Toby liked no part of this.

"Run ahead and lower the tailgate, I'll have no more trouble with him now." Muriel pulled and scolded, but the wise old horse held his ground.

"Hang onto him, Toby," she ordered. "I'll find a way to persuade him. He always was a stubborn brute." She opened the trunk of her new car and thrown in behind some large cans of paint she found a hunt whip. "He'll change his mind when he feels this." The enraged girl took the whip and hit the horse across his rear legs. Surprised by the pain, Harlequin jumped. "Pull him! Pull him into the trailer," she screamed. The whip again whistled down on his white legs. Harlequin whinnied in terror. Even in the dark, Toby could see the fear in his eyes.

Somehow they got the plunging horse into the trailer. His white socks were spotted with blood. A long cut spurted over his eye and his body was covered with sweat. He coughed long and hard.

As Muriel tightened the catch on the tailgate, she lost all control. "If I can't have him, nobody will," she sobbed. "I'll kill him first!"

"You'll what?" Toby was finally catching on.

A dog began to howl as they put the car in gear, and rolled down the driveway. Muriel sat huddled in a corner staring ahead. As they neared the main road Toby stopped. He put on the brake and, turning to her, he said, "I don't know what you're up to, Muriel, but whatever it is, it's not for me. I've had enough of this sneaking around. From here on in, you're on your own."

He opened the car door and before Muriel could pull herself together, walked down the road.

"Toby, Toby, you've got to help me!" she called after him. "You can't walk out on me like this." But he didn't turn around.

For a long time she just sat. In the trailer Harlequin kicked and coughed. "Cut your racket," she finally yelled, banging the partition with her fist. Slowly she slid over into the driver's seat, released the brake, and headed for the Tappan Zee bridge.

At Applebee Farm, Willy comforted Wendy. "Cheer up, Wen," he said, "it's impossible to disappear with a horse in this day and age. The police will catch up with Muriel and maybe we'll still get to Piping Rock on time."

However, Mrs. Fleming knew better. She called her mother, and cancelled the elaborate plans for the Long Island excursion.

" 'If the police don't find our horse soon, I'll hire my

own detectives,' " Mrs. Fleming quoted her mother as saying. But even the thought of Granny Babcock with a fleet of private eyes could not make Wendy smile.

"That fink! Sis knew she was up to no good," Robin kept repeating to herself. "But we'll find her. She can't get away with this." Robin sounded very positive, but it was clear that she had no inside information.

"Put some clothes on Wen, and we'll scour the country some more. Willy knew that nothing was worse than sitting still. They crisscrossed the county in the Volvo. They checked every riding stable and barn. The police got to work in earnest, but by the end of the week Muriel and Harlequin were still missing. The newspapers got hold of the story, and Harlequin's picture was splashed across the tabloids. The local radio station even interviewed Wendy.

"What can Muriel do with him?" mused Willy. "She can't ride him and he must be harder to hide than the Hope Diamond." By now everyone knew of the white-faced horse with the pale blue eyes.

Mrs. Fleming, though she was desperately upset about Wendy, still had time to feel sorry for the Alexanders.

"Right or wrong, they're trying," she insisted. "They must be worried to death about Muriel."

Two days later the phone rang. "Muriel's home," said the highly agitated voice on the other end of the line. "She's very sick. You won't press charges, will you?" Grace Alexander implored.

"And the horse? Where's the horse?" George Fleming asked her.

"We don't know. She won't tell us a thing. We called

our doctor for Muriel and he has advised us to consult a psychiatrist. We have no other hope."

"Those poor people and that unfortunate child. I would hate to press charges. Making trouble for them won't get Harlequin back," Margaret Fleming said, as she discussed the situation with her husband.

"But my horse? What's happened to my horse?" Wendy asked. She still found it difficult to extend any sympathy to the Alexanders.

Another week passed, but Muriel remained silent. She was placed in a sanatorium under a psychiatrist's care, and Harlequin was still missing.

The police had done their utmost, but murders, bank robberies, and kidnappings took precedence over the theft of a horse. Only Wendy and Will persisted.

"What would you say to paying Muriel a visit?" Will suggested.

"Would they let us in?" Wendy asked. She was all for the idea.

Willy spread a large-scale map of Westchester and adjoining counties in front of him. Marked in red were the stables they had visited.

"It looks impressive," he said, pointing to the rash of red, "but actually we've accomplished nothing." He did not hide the discouragement in his voice.

Wendy, studying the map over his shoulder, agreed. "Muriel is the key," she said. "If we approach her right she might tell us something." She thought a moment. Then she said, "You know Will, sometimes I feel so angry at Muriel and at other times I really feel sorry for her. Whatever possessed her to steal Harley? I guess there really is something wrong with her."

Will was more concerned about Harlequin. "If she doesn't give us a clue, we're licked," he said. "We can't visit every barn in the country before school begins." What had started as an adventure for the boy was becoming a discouraging chore. The weather was hot and humid, and the Tweeds' swimming pool was much more inviting that the seemingly hopeless search for Harlequin. But his loyalty to Wendy made him continue the hunt. Muriel was their best chance.

Several days later Wendy and Will drove to Fair Winds Sanatorium. To a casual observer it had the appearance of a palatial summer resort, but Wendy felt a shudder as the nurse led them through the cold, impersonal lounges and hallways to Muriel's room. She saw one well-dressed patient sitting at a table, staring at a partially completed jigsaw puzzle. Another slept in front of a blaring television set. In one corner sat a very old woman, huddled in a wheel chair.

Muriel's appearance was the greatest shock. If the nurse had not said, "I've brought someone to see you, Muriel," Wendy and Will would not have recognized the girl seated in the wicker chair, staring vacantly into space. She was clean and neatly dressed now, but her pale, drawn face was completely expressionless.

"Hello, Muriel." Wendy spoke first, trying to break the ice. The girl made no reply. Her once tangled hair was brushed into a neat pageboy. But her face, no longer disgruntled looking, was blank, and her large brown eyes were dull.

That's not Muriel, Wendy wanted to say, but she kept silent.

"We need your help, Muriel." Will spoke earnestly to the girl. "You might even feel better yourself if you help us." He sounded more convincing than he felt.

"Try to talk with them, they're your friends," the nurse added helpfully.

"I can't help anyone and no one can help me," said the girl. They had never heard such a hopeless voice.

"But you can. You must!" Wendy put an imploring hand on Muriel's shoulder. "You must help us find Harley! You love him too."

As if the human touch had opened a floodgate, Muriel began to talk in short, jerky sentences. Though much of it was incoherent, some of it made sense.

"My parents hate me," she began. "They buy me things to shut me up, but they don't love me. They wish I were dead."

"You know that's not true." Wendy didn't know what else to say.

"You have everything," she said, looking at Wendy for the first time. "Your family loves you. Your sister admires you, and now you ride my horse better than I ever did. It's just not fair!

"I'm nothing but a burden to my folks." The girl was sobbing now. "I thought I could count on Toby. The fraternity weekends were such fun. But he left me. He walked out on me when I needed him the most. In the middle of the night, he checked out and I had to drive that blasted horse across the bridge alone..."

"What bridge?" Will asked.

"The Tappan, Tappan..."

"Tappan Zee bridge?"

Muriel nodded, and fell silent.

12

The visit to Muriel had a most sobering effect on both Wendy and Will. "I thought Muriel was just a spoiled brat and a downright thief, but she's really all mixed up. She's sick, really sick!" Wendy told her mother as the three of them studied the map in Applebee Farm's living room. Mrs. Fleming had volunteered to help ferret out stables on the other side of the Tappan Zee bridge.

"Perhaps we can help with her recovery," Margaret Fleming suggested.

"How?" Wendy sounded only vaguely interested.

"I don't really know. Perhaps Muriel's doctor will have a suggestion," said Mrs. Fleming thoughtfully. "He was right when he said that you and Will might start her talking about herself."

"Let's worry about Muriel after we've found Harley," Will said.

"Will's right, Mom," Wendy agreed. "Let's find Harley first." Mrs. Fleming knew she couldn't argue with that decision.

"Why didn't we think of looking for Harley on the other side of the river? That wasn't very smart of us," Wendy said, poring over the map.

"There was no reason to," said Will. "But now that we know, we can comb the west side of the river." Muriel's admission had put fresh energy into the team of Wendy and Will.

There was only a week left before school started. Early each morning they set off in Will's car. They crossed the long bridge over the Hudson, and thoroughly searched the area. Neither had ever realized so many stables existed. A few were fancy clubs and riding academies, some were dude ranches, but the majority were second-rate, hack stables.

Every once in a while they heard of a white-faced horse, but when they tracked him down, it was never Harlequin.

Willy's persistence amazed Wendy. She had thought the horse meant nothing to him. The glamour of the chase had long since worn off and still he volunteered to drive her around. He really was great.

Will yawned as they drove into the last stable for the day. Wendy took pity on her faithful driver. "Don't get out, I can look around by myself. This place looks too crummy even for Muriel."

A huge manure pile was the first thing she noticed as she got out of the car. Off to one corner was a small red barn, the paint peeling off in strips. A rocky paddock, surrounded by broken down post-and-rail fencing made up the rest of the establishment. The place was deserted and smelled as if no one had cleaned it in months. Eight or ten mangy horses stuck their heads out of the stalls to took at Wendy, but as usual, the familiar white face was not among them. The smell of the manure hit Wendy's nostrils. She grimaced and turned to walk back to the car. "This is the worst-kept, most run down place we've..." she began.

A shrill whinny interrupted her. It came from the end stall. Wendy looked around. The horse kicked at the door and continued to whinny.

"What's the matter with that brute?" Willy had heard the racket and gotten out of the car. "What does that black scarecrow want?"

Wendy opened the stall and walked in. The moth-eaten black came over and nuzzled her pocket. A deep rasping cough made his sides heave.

"Will, Will, could he be Harlequin? Look at those blue eyes and the bumps on his legs."

"But he's black."

Wendy ran her hand over his stiff, rusty-looking coat. "I do believe it's paint." Wendy peered more closely. "It must be Harley!" She was ashamed of herself. Her pet had known her, but she had not recognized him. There were tears in her eyes as she hugged and kissed the old horse. He appeared equally delighted as he breathed softly down Wendy's neck. While feeding him a pocketful of sugar, she touched his skinny frame. His coat was dark as soot—even his white face was muddy black.

"What have they done to you, old fella?" Wendy asked her once beautiful horse.

Harley coughed long and hard.

"He sure looks terrible," Will said. "His ribs show,

he's full of sores, he's coughing his lungs out, and his color . . ."

"Poor old Harley." Wendy wanted to cry again, but she swallowed her tears. "We've found him. That's the important part. We'll call Dad and he can bring the trailer over. In the meantime, let's take Harley out of this filthy stall and find some grass for him to nibble on. Most of these poor animals look as if they haven't had a decent meal in years."

The hack stable's owner was reasonably cooperative when Mr. Fleming and the trailer arrived. He told them that early one morning about a month ago, he had found a girl and a nondescript black horse waiting for him. The girl departed saying that she would be back to ride the horse the following day. She never returned. The address she gave was false and by now she owed a good-sized board bill.

It all sounded fishy, but as the bowlegged little man made no attempt to stop them from taking the horse, Mr. Fleming said little.

"Didn't he see the photos of Harley in the newspaper?" Wendy wanted to know on the way home.

"The pictures in the paper were of a white-faced horse. The one that was brought to his stable was a seedy black," Willy interjected. "But where and how did Muriel paint him?"

"The police said something about paint cans in the trunk of the car. Muriel must have stopped some place and slopped black paint over him. It wasn't a very convincing job, but I guess the likes of that stableman don't ask too many questions." George Fleming concentrated on his driving. He was glad that Harley was found, but would the horse, at his age, be able to recover from such an ordeal? It was a good thing that Margaret had called Dr. Wallace before he left. The vet would be able to advise them.

The whole family was on hand to greet Harley as the caravan pulled into Applebee Farm's stable yard.

"He's back, he's back!" shouted Robin and Janie in unison, but Mrs. Fleming, Gran and Dr. Wallace watched silently as Willy lowered the tailgate. Wendy unhooked his headcollar and as she guided him down the ramp, he pricked up his ears and whinnied loud and clear. Georgetown answered his call and Foxy and Hippo joined in. Dragging Wendy along, Harley headed for his stall. If anything, he looked even worse than when they found him, but his step was jaunty and his blue eyes were clear and inquisitive. At his stall he hesitated, then lunged in. He buried his nose in his manger, and hungrily wolfed the food Robin had mixed for him.

Dr. Wallace let him finish his feed and then Wendy brought him out into the yard.

"What have they done to our horse, what have they done to him?" Gran exclaimed in a shocked voice. The last time she had seen him, Harlequin was a handsome chestnut with a snowy white face and legs. What she saw now was a bedraggled, black skeleton, ready for the glue factory. "Perhaps Dr. Wallace will tell us to put him to sleep." Her eyes brimmed with tears. Why did I ever get Wendy mixed up in this mess. I thought I was doing her a favor, but I certainly wasn't, she thought. Granny pulled out her handkerchief. She no longer could hold back her tears.

"Pull yourself together, Mother." Margaret Fleming knew that sympathy was no good at a time like this. "Do you want the children to see you? Why jump to conclusions? Let's wait to hear what the Doctor has to say." But the vet was silent. He walked around the horse, first looking at his heaving sides, then at his eyes, his scratched up legs, and finally passing his hand over his streaked, straw-like coat.

After ten or fifteen minutes, which seemed more like hours, Dr. Wallace finally spoke. "It's not as bad as it looks," he said. Granny sat down hard on the mounting block. Mom breathed a sigh of relief. Robin and Janie jumped up and down. But Wendy said nothing. She held her horse and waited tensely.

"His breathing will improve as soon as he is put on the correct feed again." Dr. Wallace chalked off the problems. "The scratches on his legs are superficial. I'll give him a shot of vitamins and leave a tonic for you to mix with his feed. It'll take time, but I think you can get him back in shape." Dr. Wallace was happy with his prognosis. Over the phone, Margaret Fleming had filled him in on the story. He had been afraid that he would find Harlequin beyond repair. "Those kids deserve something better than that," he had told his wife as he picked up his bag to drive over to the Flemings. "They really love that old fellow and he's done awfully well for them."

"Will I be able to ride him at the Garden?" asked Wendy in a small voice.

Dr. Wallace looked thoughtful. "That's only a month off." He hesitated. "I don't want to promise anything, but I'd give it a fifty-fifty chance."

"How do we get the paint off?" asked Robin. "We can't let him walk around looking like this."

The adults smiled at her.

Dr. Wallace considered the problem. "You'll have to take it off gradually," he said. "You can probably use turpentine on his body providing you apply it to a small section at a time and then wash it off carefully with soap and water. If you don't, you'll burn his skin off."

Willy whistled through his teeth at the job they had ahead of them.

"But what about his face?" Margaret Fleming had visions of a chestnut horse with four white stockings and a dirty black face cantering around the ring at Madison Square Garden. "What do we do with his face?"

"Turp is too strong for that." The doctor appeared stymied.

"If he doesn't know who does," said Wendy quietly to Will.

"How about asking the druggist?" Janie Tweed piped up. "My mother's hair is a different color every year. She must use something to get rid of the stuff before she puts the new color on."

The adults had a problem keeping a straight face, except Gran who said, "That's a very smart idea, Janie. I'd leave the poor horse in peace today, but tomorrow we'll pay the druggist a visit."

13

"It's useful to have a sister who drives," said Robin the following morning, as she parked herself in the front seat of the old station wagon.

"Glad to be appreciated." Wendy smiled ruefully to herself as she remembered her problems in getting a learner's permit. But now with her junior license in her pocket, she and Robin could go places. The place they were going this Saturday morning was the local drug store to learn about paint and dye removers.

"I don't know much about horses and paint," said the druggist. "But when women who have hair dyed black decide to be blondes, I have several preparations to offer them."

Wendy, already reading the directions on one of the bottles, frowned worriedly. "This stuff only removes dye; what we need is a paint remover."

"Maybe it'll remove both?" Robin didn't sound too convincing.

"Besides, it's much too expensive! We'd need at least ten bottles. Where would we find thirty dollars?"

"Granny, of course!"

"No!" said Wendy emphatically. "Harlequin's cost Granny enough already."

Robin, thoughtfully chewing a penny's worth of bubble gum, came up with an answer. "How about buying a bottle to try on Harlequin's face? We could use turpentine for the rest of his body. That's cheap enough!"

"Not a bad idea, girls." The druggist approved Robin's logic. "See how it works. You can always come back for more."

Equipped with their expensive color remover and a large can of turpentine, the girls set to work. Harlequin was so happy to have someone fuss over him again that he stood still willingly.

"This stuff says, make one application, then cover head with hot towels, after ten minutes rinse!" Wendy looked puzzled.

"I'll get the hot towels while you smear the goo on," Robin volunteered and disappeared into the tack room. "Be careful of Harlequin's eyes. Don't drip remover into them."

Wendy, insulted at her sister's lack of confidence, turned her back and petted her horse. "Sorry to put you through this, old boy," she said sympathetically as she applied remover to Harlequin's face. "Soon you'll be yourself again."

As if to say "yes," Harlequin stamped his foot.

Wendy rubbed the smelly stuff into the horse's face

and then called Robin, "Get a move on with the hot towels!"

"Keep your shirt on!" Robin yelled, as she brought two steaming towels and helped Wendy hold them on Harlequin's face.

The horse liked no part of it, but the girls talked soothingly to him, and he submitted to the indignity.

"I hate to look!" said Wendy, pulling off the now cool towel.

"Don't!" Robin knew how anxious her sister must be. "I'll look first." And while Wendy was gathering her courage, she quickly sponged off Harlequin's face.

"It hasn't done a thing!"

"I thought as much," said Wendy, in a discouraged tone of voice. "We've got to find something that removes ordinary house paint and that still won't remove Harley's skin and hair."

"I think I've found it for you girls." Wendy and Robin had been so intent on their experiment that they had not heard Willy drive up.

"I was speaking to a friend of mine who worked at odd jobs last summer," the boy explained. "He painted a neighbor's fence and of course got the stuff all over himself. Al knew he was allergic to turp, but he found that kerosene took paint off his hands and hardly burned at all."

"That just might work! Sometimes you make a lot of sense," Wendy said, and smiled at her friend.

"But don't forget to wash it off with soap and water," Will said, sounding a trifle superior as he deposited a gallon of kerosene in the stable yard.

"Of course!" Wendy answered, spiritedly.

After Will had left she said, "Should we start now?"
She eyed the can doubtfully.

"We've put him through enough for now," said Robin.
"Let's work on his body after lunch."

"That's a good idea," Wendy agreed. "I'll give him
some grass." With her arm around her horse she walked
him down the lane toward the paddock.

That afternoon, rag in hand, the two girls started to
rub his rump. The old horse shifted his weight. The
rubbing was all right, but he objected to the smell of
kerosene.

"He doesn't like it much, but it works!" cried Robin,
triumphantly. "His rear is two-toned now. If we do a little
every day for the next month he might look okay again.
But the smell . . ."

"He'll put up with it. He's a good old trooper," said
Wendy, petting her horse. "But . . ." Suddenly the reac-
tion set in. She sat down on the mounting block and,
utterly dejected, she cried, "It's all so hopeless! I have to
go back to school tomorrow and the National Horse Show
is only three weeks away."

Robin, walking Harlequin, thought hard.

"I guess I should just be thankful that he's back,"
Wendy said, and sniffed. She was feeling ashamed of herself.

Suddenly, Robin said eagerly, "We can do it!"

"How?" Wendy asked, still feeling disconsolate.

"I'll be here. What's the matter with my getting Harlequin back in shape? Or don't you think I can do it?" she
added, a trifle belligerently.

"Sure! But what about Georgetown? You can't have
time to work two horses after school." Although she didn't

show it, Wendy was bowled over by Robin's generous offer.

Robin stuck her hands in her pockets. "It's like this, Wen," she said, looking as nonchalant as possible. "If we can get Harlequin back in shape before the Garden, he stands a good chance of being in the ribbons. Georgetown still lacks experience. Next year is time enough for him."

"Do you really mean it?"

"Sure." Robin shifted from one foot to the other. Wendy's look of gratitude embarrassed her a little.

"I'll make it up to you, I promise."

"Stop worrying! It will be fun to work Harlequin."

Robin would get the job done. Wendy was sure of that. She could see it in her eyes.

The entries for the National Horse Show at Madison Square Garden had closed several weeks before. But with the help of a sympathetic member of the executive committee, Harlequin's name was added to the already huge junior working hunter division. Georgetown was scratched from the ranks of the large hunter ponies. Snooks had never been entered. Janie had long since decided that it was far better to enjoy herself and watch the largest show in the country than have a super attack of horse show nerves.

When Muriel's case came up in Children's Court, she was placed in her psychiatrist's custody at his request. Her parents reimbursed the Flemings and Mrs. Babcock for expenses incurred in Harlequin's abduction. The Austin Healey was sold to pay court costs and Muriel's weekly sanitarium bills.

Although Muriel would be in a nursing home for the

best part of a year, her doctor was optimistic about her recovery.

Robin was in her element. Each day, as soon as the school bus dropped her at the gate, she rushed to the house, pulled on her jeans, and was off to the stable.

On most days she worked first with the kerosene rag and then rode. With four meals a day, large doses of tender loving care and regular exercise, Harlequin was beginning to look like a horse again. His color was still muddy, but the sheen was coming back to his coat, and flesh was starting to cover his hatrack-like rump. Even his cough was better.

Robin exercised him systematically. She limbered him up with walking, encouraged him to trot to build muscle, added suppling exercises to make him handy, and as an occasional treat for herself, included a course of jumps.

Working Harlequin was no hardship for her but, once in a while, when the weather was extra nasty or when she had a heavy load of homework, the project lost its glamour. Why am I killing myself to get a horse ready for Wendy to show at the Garden? she'd ask herself angrily. But when she made her weekly call to her sister at boarding school, she had only praise for Harlequin and enthusiasm for his progress.

"You're a good girl, Rob," her father told her. "I'm proud of you."

Mom beamed and Gran called her the assistant horse trainer. As the junior weekend of the National Horse Show came closer however, Robin sometimes regretted her noble gesture.

Georgetown had been roughed and Robin only had

time for him on weekends. But ready or not, it would have been fun to take him to the Garden. This way she did all the work and Wendy would have the glory. What had her sister meant when she had said she would make it up to her? Robin wondered. By now she had probably forgotten that she ever made such a statement.

14

"Robin and Harlequin look pretty sharp," said Wendy, as she surveyed the country's top junior hunters walking around Madison Square Garden's oval ring.

Gran nodded in agreement and beamed at her box full of guests. They were all watching the under saddle class, judged on way of moving and manners. A working hunter class and a $1,000 junior working hunter stake would make up the division. Wendy would be aboard for these.

Wendy had invited Robin to ride her beautiful horse in the hack class. This was her way of thanking her sister for getting Harlequin ready for the Garden.

"I had a letter from Muriel, yesterday. I think you'll want to see it, Gran," Wendy said, and quietly slipped the envelope to her grandmother. It was too personal a note, Wendy felt, to broadcast its contents. Her parents had seen it, and now Gran. Somehow Wendy understood the effort it must have caused Muriel to write this scribbled letter.

It began:

"Dear Wendy,

"I'm sorry I caused all of you so much trouble, but I hated everyone and I wanted to hurt all of you. I don't quite know why I stole Harlequin, but perhaps someday I'll understand that too. I'm still pretty mixed up, but hearing that you found him makes me feel a whole lot better. I felt awful about what I did to that old horse. Good luck at the Garden. If you win anything, please send me a picture.

Your friend,
Muriel"

Mrs. Babcock looked thoughtful as she returned the envelope to Wendy. "I don't know very much about this sort of thing, dear, but I have a feeling that Muriel is on the road to recovery."

Wendy nodded. "Perhaps when Muriel gets out of the home, I could invite her over to ride."

"That would be very nice." Gran Babcock had trouble keeping her voice steady.

Wendy pocketed the letter and concentrated on the arena.

"They're asking them to trot now!" exclaimed Janie Tweed breathlessly. Perched on the edge of her seat in Box Ten, she looked less chunky in her navy blue Sunday coat, but her face sported the same saucy expression, and her pigtails bounced jauntily on her well-tailored shoulders.

Robin was 100 percent business in the ring. Never in

her fondest dreams had she imagined her reward would be this great. In return, she would give Harlequin the best ride ever. She sat up straighter than straight, talked soothingly to her horse, and kept her eyes peeled for interference. Even in a ring as big as Madison Square Garden, forty nervous horses could cause quite a rumpus.

At the beginning of the class, she walked Harlequin quietly, getting him used to his strange surroundings. At the command of "trot," he moved him out. He had a wonderful springy gait, and she wanted the judges to notice him. With this many horses to consider, there was always a chance of being overlooked.

"Robin's making sure that the judges see her," Willy observed. He preferred the Garden when the Toronto Maple Leafs were playing, but today he was rooting for Harlequin.

"They're cantering now." It was the first time that Granny Babcock had relaxed sufficiently to sit back in her comfortable upholstered seat.

A box at Madison Square Garden for Junior Weekend was hard to obtain, but Granny had somehow wangled one. With her family and Janie and Willy Tweed around her, and her horse in the ring, she sat proudly watching her granddaughter. In the last few months she had learned what was expected of hunter type show horses and smiled patiently at the naïve questions her old lady friends asked her. She found it hard to believe that luncheons and bridge parties had ever been her whole life. Young people and horses were far more interesting.

"Robin's riding on a loose rein," Mrs. Fleming said, sitting in the back of the box. She breathed a long sigh of relief.

"If she'd tightened up on him he'd probably take off with her." Wendy, remembering her first ride on Harley, was most impressed with her sister's skill.

"Working Harlequin has improved her horsemanship, but both of you have learned far more than riding. . . ." George Fleming squeezed Wendy's hand affectionately. "I'm proud of you two."

"And it's been great for Granny too," Wendy whispered to her mother.

"Line up!" came the command from the ring. "Will the following ten horses stay in, please." Harlequin's number was called third.

"Look!" Janie giggled. "Harlequin just shook all the powder off his forehead."

"Drat!" Wendy looked upset. "Will the judges count off for that? We had to use baby powder to cover that awful greenish look."

"Of course not!" Mr. Fleming said confidently. Robin's scrubbing in recent weeks had paid off. If you didn't look too closely, both Harlequin's stockings and face were white again. The crash feeding program had also worked. He had put on weight, and his chestnut body looked sleek and well cared for.

With so few horses left in the ring, the judges could pick out the six ribbon winners. First they asked all to walk, trot, and canter. Then six at a time were asked to hand gallop.

Harlequin broke stride once when an unruly gray came too close, but the judges' backs were turned, and Robin prayed they hadn't seen it.

At the command to hand gallop, Robin let Harlequin stretch his legs. He coughed once as she leaned forward, tightened her reins a touch, and let him run. The horse whose number had been called in second place bucked, a bay galloped on the wrong lead, and another tried to kick. Robin used her head and kept Harlequin clear of other horses. She let him tear on the straight away, eating up the ring in long smooth strides, but she remembered to steady him on the turns. At the command of "Halt!" Robin brought her weight back in the saddle and in a stage whisper said, "Whoa!" Harlequin stopped so suddenly that if her seat had not been tight, she would have gone over his head. The judges noted their prompt halt and were looking at them when Robin dropped her reins on Harlequin's neck. This extra bit of showmanship proved that the horse who, seconds before, had been galloping was now perfectly relaxed.

The judges marked their cards, handed them to the ringmaster, and left the arena. Wendy held her breath. Granny's red plush seat groaned as she shifted her considerable weight. There were tiny beads of perspiration on her forehead.

Finally the P.A. system crackled. "We have the results of class 101—junior working hunters under saddle. First, number 189, Gay Girl—owned by..."

Wendy looked crestfallen.

"Second, number 270, Harlequin—owned by Mrs. George Babcock and ridden by Robin Fleming."

Box Ten cheered loudly! Robin had done it! She had ridden Harlequin to a coveted second place.

"I hope I can do as well," said Wendy in a small voice, "school hasn't helped my riding any."

"Of course you can," Willy encouraged her. "Just play it cool."

While Robin slid off Harlequin at the out gate and walked toward the head of the ramp, Wendy ran down to congratulate her sister. First she hugged and kissed her horse, then she thumped Robin on the back. "You did it! You did it!" was all she could say.

Harley stamped his foot and nickered. *I* did it, he seemed to insist.

"You're right!" Robin agreed with him as she reached in her pocket for a handful of sugar. Harlequin's blue eyes zeroed in and he gobbled the slightly soiled lumps. "We won forty dollars. Isn't he wonderful!" Robin was too stunned to talk much, but it was easy to see that this was the most exciting day of her life.

Arm in arm, the two girls walked down the ramp. Harlequin, his red ribbon still fluttering proudly from his brow band, every so often nudged one of them in the small of the back. I want more sugar, he seemed to say.

But Wendy only laughed. "You've had enough for now, old man. You'll get more later."

As they neared the stable area, the air became warm and stuffy. The girls, not used to what greeted them, stared wide-eyed at the hundreds of temporary stalls which stretched over Madison Square Garden. There were rows and rows of horses, narrow aisles covered with wet matting, and every few minutes a recording of the fire chief's voice. "Absolutely no smoking, absolutely no smoking!"

The girls took Harlequin's tack off, gave him a sip of water, and rubbed his back dry. "Your class won't be called for half an hour. Let him rest and we'll look around." Robin could sense that Wendy's horse show nerves were beginning to tighten.

"Okay," Wendy answered. But she had lost some of her bounce.

The wet matting squelched under their boots as they walked down the aisles. Most of the horses had the same temporary stalls as Harlequin, but the big stables glamourized their quarters by covering every box with stable colors. The tack rooms were magnificent. All had handsome bridle and saddle racks, fancy mirrors, and neat cots for grooms to sleep in. Some even had horsy chandeliers, clothes closets, carpets, radios, and TV's.

"They're pretty snaky, aren't they?" Robin commented, perfectly relaxed. It was Wendy's turn to have the butterflies.

"We'd better give Harley some cough medicine."

"You give it to him." Wendy's nerves were getting to her.

Robin took the bottle out of the tack trunk, tilted Harley's head up and stuck the flask in the side of his mouth. Like the good old trooper he was, he took a slug and swallowed it. Robin wiped his mouth with a tissue and stuck it back in her pocket.

"I want to take a practice jump," Wendy said. She could stand it no longer. She climbed aboard and made her way to the rickety obstacle set up at the base of the ramp. Six or seven juniors were there ahead of her. This made Wendy all the more nervous. When her turn came, her knees were shaking. But Harlequin was calm, and he jogged over the little fence as if he had been at Applebee Farm.

"Buck up, Sis. There's nothing to worry about." Robin

gave her sister's black boots a final wipe, checked Harlequin's girth, and walked up the ramp with them. "I'll give your number to the starter and go back to the box. I don't want to miss Harlequin's round."

Wendy nodded silently.

"When you get in there, remember to send him," were Robin's parting words. She stopped on the stairs leading to the boxes and stared down at the mass of horses and riders milling around. It looked wild, but Robin would have given anything to be there. At the same moment, Wendy would gladly have changed places with her.

"I hope Harlequin doesn't get kicked," Robin said, and collapsed in one of the comfortable box seats. "It's bedlam down there."

Janie was studying the program intently. "Fifty horses are entered in the small junior working hunter class."

"And they're all at the in gate. Wendy will be out of the mob soon. I saw to that. She's number ten to go."

Harlequin did not mind the pushing and shoving. Only Wendy was congealed with fright. A martyr about to be thrown to the lions could not have felt worse. And the spectators at the Coliseum could never have made more noise than the capacity crowd which thronged Madison Square Garden.

A couple of horses refused. One girl fell off, and then the horse in front of her entered the ring. "Number 270 get ready," said the starter, and Wendy tried to pull herself together. She pushed her hunt cap down hard on her head. Her legs felt miles away, but as the in gate opened, Harlequin carried her into the ring. Wendy remembered Robin's words. "Send him," she had said, and by gosh she would.

In an almost trancelike state, she trotted, cantered a circle, and then headed for the first brush fence. Harlequin took a tremendous leap and galloped toward the wall. Instead of steadying him, Wendy gunned her willing horse, and he jumped off three legs.

"She's running him off his feet!" hissed Robin.

"That's better than hanging back," Janie replied. She always saw the bright side.

Granny gripped the arms of her chair. Margaret Fleming grabbed her husband's arm and said, "She's riding dangerously."

Wendy was in a daze, and only Harlequin's jumping ability saved them from complete disaster.

"You told me to send him," was Wendy's only comment as she returned to the box. She was close to tears.

"But you forgot to steady him around the turns," Robin commented. "Let's sit here and watch the rounds carefully. That way you'll find out where you should send and where you have to steady." But to Janie she whispered, "Darn it! There goes our chance for the championship. Wish I could have ridden him!"

Gran hid her disappointment well and was soon organizing lunch. "I'm treating you all to the horse show luncheon party. I think we should go now, so we'll get back in time for Wendy's stake class."

Everyone but Wendy was anxious to walk over to the elegant buffet. "I think I'd rather stay here," she said quietly. "I'm not hungry."

"I'll keep her company," Will offered. To pass up good food was a major sacrifice for Willy. "I'll buy Wen a hot dog," he promised Mrs. Babcock as the family filed out of the box on their way to lunch.

"Do you think I should let Robin ride Harlequin in the stake class?" Wendy asked as soon as the others had left. "It's a crime to mess up a good horse." Her large brown eyes, brimming with tears, looked imploringly at her friend. "You've got to tell me the truth."

"Don't you dare!" he answered her firmly. "Just because Robin did a good job in the hack class does not mean she can do the same over fences. You're over your stage fright now. In the next class use your head and ride. I'll put my money on you any day."

Wendy could have kissed him, but she did not think that Box Ten at the Garden was quite the place. Instead she gave his hand a squeeze. "I stopped you from having a great lunch," she said apologetically. "You didn't have to stay with me."

"I wanted to." Willy gave Wendy the benefit of his irresistible crooked grin. "Come feed me, woman. I'd like some hot dogs even if you don't."

By the time they returned from filling up Willy and paying a visit to the lobby booths, the crowd was beginning to return. Throngs of children and their parents were filing in to see the afternoon competitions. Business was brisk for the program-sellers and the ice-cream and popcorn vendors. In the arena the jump crew was setting up the stake course. There were forty horses in the small division and fifty or more in the large group, so more than ninety juniors would compete for the $1,000 Junior Working Hunter Stake.

Wendy knew the jumps by heart, but this time she would stand on the stairs by the gate and watch the other horses. There was no hurry to fetch Harlequin. She would ride near the end of the class.

When the pink coated ringmaster blew his coaching horn and the first rider entered the ring, Wendy was ready. Leaning against the stair rail she analyzed each performance. By the time the class was over she knew how many strides a horse had to take to meet the obstacle correctly. Well satisfied, she walked down the ramp to fetch Harlequin.

The crowd at the in gate had thinned, and they stood in comfort to await their turn.

"I think you'll see a difference," Willy promised Mrs. Babcock. To prove his point, Wendy entered the arena looking confident. She circled her horse at a collected canter and let him increase slightly for the first brush fence. Five strides to the post-and-rail she said to herself, and Harlequin met it perfectly. Now, she thought, across the diagonal and over the white gate. Wendy sat down and rode. It was a long stretch, and she was not going to let Harlequin pick up speed. One stride away from the fence, she clucked and he took off. Now steady him up the other side for the wall and the in-and-out. Ten thousand people were watching her, but they no longer worried Wendy. Her mind was on giving Harlequin the best ride possible.

In Box Ten Janie was pinching Robin with excitement. Granny Babcock, leaning over the edge of the box, was in danger of falling out. Only Will was calm. He sat pridefully with an "of course she's going to win" expression on his face.

The feeling of controlled power thrilled Wendy. Harlequin moved like a smooth machine ready to do her bidding. If she squeezed with her legs he increased, and if she sat down in the saddle and took a feel of his mouth, he came back to her. When they jumped Wendy felt as though they were flying. She wished the course was twice as long. It would all be over too soon. Almost regretfully she steered across the final diagonal and cleared the aiken. Six strides later she asked for a big fence over the gray chicken coop. Harlequin obliged, and they soared over amid deafening applause.

"That was a brilliant round!" George Fleming was the first to find his voice. Robin and Janie jumped up on their seats and clapped wildly. Granny and Mom hugged each other.

Wendy stayed aboard Harlequin. She wanted to be near the gate when they called the horses for soundness. She knew her round had been a good one.

The judges debated forever. It was hard to score a class of ninety. Finally they signed their cards and handed them to the ringmaster. He relayed their decision via walkie-talkie to the announcer.

"Will the following horses come in for soundness please: 270, 184, 111, 56 . . ." Ten horses were called. Wendy and Harlequin entered the ring first. She had dismounted, pulled up her stirrups, and put her reins over her horse's head. At the ringmaster's nod she jogged Harlequin past the judges, 184 followed, and so did the rest. When the dust cleared, and a red carpet had been rolled over the tanbark, a smiling lady presented Wendy with a huge silver cup. Wendy tried to thank her, but words were hard to find. She wanted to thank everybody from Harlequin himself, to Granny—even Muriel— and of course Will, who had made her ride as she had never ridden before.

In Box Ten Robin was counting points. "We're champion, small junior working hunter champion at Madison Square Garden!" she whooped. "Harlequin has eight points and the nearest horse has only six!"

"He's won $340!" Janie was wide-eyed with admiration.

"We can never repay him for what he's done for all of us," Mom said. Her eyes were moist.

And Mr. Fleming added, "Applebee Farm is his home for life."

Will disappeared to help Wendy with Harlequin while Granny held court.

"My father always prided himself on being a good judge of horse flesh. I must have inherited that from him." She winked broadly at Mom. "And I'm a good judge of riders, too," she added.

The Flemings, Gran, the Tweeds, and Harley all rode home together. It was a tight squeeze for the human passengers, but Harley rode in style. His legs were well bandaged with heavy cotton, his tail was wrapped against rubbing, and on his back was his beautiful new cooler. Robin had sneaked a hay net in to him. Hay is *verboten* for heavey horses, but Robin wanted to give him a treat. Munching happily, the champ rode home to Applebee Farm.

While Mom fixed a late supper, the young Flemings and Tweeds made Harley comfortable. To make his bed doubly soft, Willy dragged an extra bale of peat moss into his stall. Robin and Janie filled his water bucket to the brim and Wendy chopped carrots into his special feed. As they said good-night to their hero, Wendy dashed into the tack room and brought out the lump sugar box. Sprinkling his feed generously with white dots she said, "You may get cavities in your teeth, but you've earned a real treat tonight." She put her arms around the old horse and hugged him. Harley, not realizing that the sugar was in his manger, snuffled around Wendy's pockets. "It's in your feed old-timer. Enjoy your dinner and have a good sleep. You deserve it."

There was a lump in Wendy's throat as she bade Harley good-night. She was close to tears, but they were tears of happiness. "They're waiting for us at the house," yelled Willy, grabbing her by the hand. Robin and Janie latched onto her other arm and the four of them ran up to the house for supper.